Hippocrene Language and Travel Guide to

AUSTRALIA

Helen Jonsen

Illustrated by John Colquhoun

HIPPOCRENE BOOKS
New York

For information, address:
HIPPOCRENE BOOKS, INC.
171 Madison Avenue
New York, NY 10016

Cataloging-in-Publication Data
Jonsen, Helen.
Hippocrene language and travel guide to Australia / Helen Jonsen ; illustrated by John Colquhoun.
p. cm.
ISBN 0-7818-0166-4
1. Australia—Guidebooks. 2. English language—Australia. 3. Australianisms. I. Title.
DU95.J66 1944
919.404'63—dc20 93-47140
CIP

Printed in the United States of America.

For my little Wallabies
Christopher and Ainsley

Dear Julian
For a friend who
enjoys language
as much as I!
All the best
Helen Jonsen

Contents

Acknowledgments

Everyone who helped set me on course writing about Australia, when I started *Kangaroo's Comments & Wallaby's Words: The Aussie Word Book* in 1983, cannot be forgotten, but the biggest thanks this time around should go to the members of our household, especially my Aussie mate, Mark, once again haunted by the phrase "The Book."

I must acknowledge Jenny, Ross, Emma, Tim and Brett for showing us a few of the lesser known but terrific family destinations around Brisbane, which we would not have found or enjoyed without them. All the Watkins have shown us places dear to them around Brisbane and the coasts. They have been very patient with all of my questions, as well as the curiosity of our newest generation.

From my heart, a very special thanks to Gladys Ritchie for sharing with us her love of Gippsland. Time and again, we have appreciated the beauty of the Land of the Lyre Bird, its hills, valleys, farms and gardens. We thank Mrs. Ritchie and many others for leaving us their legacy at Coal Creek, the historical mining town re-creation.

Thanks again to John Colquhoun for adding his creative energies to the project—coming up with clever witty illustrations about the Land Down Under. Additional thanks to A.J. Jacobson for helping me become more computer literate and getting this project onto disk.

Let me credit the Mount Vernon Public Library for extended use of other books and periodicals and the

Library of the Australian Consulate in New York which helped with some of the most up-to-date research questions.

A final note of thanks to all the readers who, like me, find Australia such a fascinating place.

—Helen Jonsen, 1994

Preface

Oz, the Land Down Under, the Antipodes, Terra Australis—no matter what you call Australia it fascinates people the world over. Starting in the eighties, it captivated America's imagination like no other place. Some blame it on the 1983 America's Cup which Australian sailors foisted after 130 years in the hands of American yachtsmen. Some say Aussie film makers captured their attention. Then a clever tourism campaign starring comedian Paul Hogan lured Americans to holiday Down Under and "throw another shrimp on the **barby**."

Perhaps, it's a sign of modern times. Twenty years ago, Australia was too far away for anyone but the wealthiest or most ardent traveler. Journeying to Oz proved impossible to squeeze into a two-week American vacation! After all, it could take two months by ship to get there from New York. Even keeping in touch with Australians was difficult. Mail could easily take three months to meander ten thousand miles around the world. In recent years things have changed! Now daily air travel, direct telephone service, facsimile machines and satellite television broadcasts shrink the distance.

Because the trip to Australia takes up to two days travel time (I'll explain more about that later) and airline tickets are in the $1,000 to $2,000 range, it is still a big decision to head Down Under, but it is certainly worth every minute and every cent of it. It is a wonderful place to visit alone and even more wonderful for families. Australians believe in leisure like no other people on earth. They think everyone deserves a good time in life everyday, not just on holidays. So for the traveler, it's imperative to have fun, to enjoy the sunshine, the sea and the beaches—the great outdoors—and the creative arts such a place breeds. To vacation Down Under is to relax, look around, enjoy. It's never a case of "It's Tuesday, it must be Brussels or another art museum."

To see Australia is a lot like seeing the United States (properly that is). You need time. When people travel to America they want to take in the big cities, some historic sights and maybe the national parks. You need time to go from place to place, to cover the thousands of miles within U.S. boundaries. You cannot see Yellowstone and Yosemite in the same day.

An Australian trip needs to stand alone, not be squeezed in between three days in New Zealand, a weekend in Bali and a side trip to Fiji. You'll need time to absorb the splendor of Sydney Harbour, the historic freshness of Melbourne, the living ocean museum of the Great Barrier Reef, the vastness of the Outback, the soothing warmth of the southern sun, the unimaginable cleanliness and welcome feeling of cities like Perth and Adelaide, as well as a chance to sample wines and savor the freshest of seafood, loll about on endless never-crowded beaches—and the list goes on.

Generally, Australians really like Americans, but they know something we don't. They watch American television and have a good ear for American-English, but we unsuspecting **Yanks** may not realize the Aussies speak a whole other version of the Queen's English. In their fun-loving way, Aussies are not above taking the **mickey out of** a novice ear.

Here's an example:

"Can I **bot a chewie**?" regardless of the accent, stands out as an odd question and the meaning will befuddle most Americans. It's the first completely Australian sentence I ever heard and it sent me looking for more. In Australian-English **bot a chewie** means "borrow a piece of chewing gum." **Chewie** is never called gum in Australia because a **gum** is a tree!

With that in mind it becomes obvious Australians speak a different brand of English than Americans do. This book will help explain the labels, words and phrases (not the accents) which might trouble someone first confronted by **fair dinkum** Aussie speech. It will offer the traveler a light-hearted look at the spoken language broadened by the customs, climate and colloquialisms adopted Down Under that are distinctly different from those used in America.

For anyone familiar with British-English, some of the phrases will not sound strange because Aussies employ many Britishisms in their day-to-day speech. The most common ones will be noted.

Many factors shaped the spoken language of Oz and her unique literature as well. Australia's isolation before mass media (prior to the 1950s and 60s) had a heavy impact and so did its early beginnings as a prison colony, home to lower classes of British society complete with the jargon and slang of the back alleys of London, Dublin and Glasgow. In addition, native aborigines salted the tongue with their words and phrases to describe the things no white man had ever seen before. It all adds up to a combination different from America's English.

The Australians call their home the Lucky Country and travelers who get the chance to tour the world's biggest island should consider themselves lucky as well. And when packing, they should not forget to pack a **swag** full of Aussie-English to enjoy the trip all the more.

How to Use This Book

As the title says, this is not just a travel book. It is a book about the *language and travel* of Australia. With "language" in equal weight with travel, the book is divided into two very distinct sections. Part I offers a comprehensive introduction to traveling in Australia. It helps choose when to go, how to go, how to travel with ease and how to find things truly Australian.

If you've looked at the contents, you know the content of the book is different from most travel guides. It focuses on kinds of travel interests and then takes you by the hand around the country to those specific places, instead of just giving you region-by-region notes and making you sort through them.

But no book about Australia should be considered complete without a discussion of the marvelous language spoken Down Under. Because so many folks assume that Australia is an English-speaking country, it must be "the 51st state." They figure it's so closely related to America that they need not know anything about the language or the culture before they get there. Wrong. Hence, Part II: Aussie Words. This section will take you by the hand through the vocabulary maze shaped by a people living too far from the Queen's English to care if anyone approved. By studying the language, we learn a lot about life. For, in words there lives history and culture.

Some details: assuming your first interest is travel, the travel part comes first—helping you plan your holiday by season or interest and giving good information on choices of carrier. Chapters 4 and 5 concentrate on family travel and offer enlightening ideas for one of the longest trips possible on the face of the globe.

In all these pages, you will find some words set in boldface—they are Aussie words—jargon, colloquialisms, euphemisms and slang. If their meanings are not immediately clear, you will encounter them again in Part II. In Part II, all Australian words and sayings will be in boldface for clarity. Most will be listed in the index to make it easy to find other references.

If you would like, read Part II first. That will give you a chance to bone up on language and culture. Then all travel details will fall into place easily. Some ideas will be repeated in each section to help the reader who is ingesting the book in small doses.

A large portion of Part II, the language section, has appeared previously in *Kangaroo's Comments & Wallaby's Words: The Aussie Word Book* (Hippocrene Books, New York: 1988). The text has been edited with additions and deletions and has been rearranged to complement the travel aspect of this publication.

Part I

Down to Oz

The Land Down Under lures so many of us to its great expanse. Many believe they will find a rugged land like America's Old West, filled with cattle, cowboys and pioneers still carving out a living in the unforgiving desert. Others believe they will find a country caught in a time warp—looking like post-World War II America, unsophisticated, out of fashion and waiting for news of the world from England and America. Even more think of Australia as a dreamland—a never-ending summer where the beach is the center of everyday life, and everyone surfs and plays topless on the sand.

How wrong and how right can we be? Are these descriptions myth or reality? I would say a bit of both. Australia is all of this rolled into one great land but it doesn't end there.

First, Australia is an urban country, with close to 90 percent of the population living in the major cities and their surrounding suburbs. That's a surprising fact for most people. The major cities of Sydney and Melbourne are as cosmopolitan as Los Angeles, San Francisco and Boston. The other mainland state capitals—Perth, Adelaide and Brisbane—have smaller populations and are more on par with Providence, San Diego or Tallahassee.

Modern high-rise buildings rub shoulders with turn-of-the-century architecture. Mass transit is well planned, clean and efficient. In Adelaide and Melbourne, tram systems complement the train and bus lines. In Sydney, ferries and water taxis move the population around the harbor area.

Beyond the cities is the **Bush**. Australia's great and

somewhat young heritage has been built on the land and on the sheep's back. **Stations** from the green lush hills of Gippsland outside of Melbourne to the unforgiving harsh plains of the Northern Territory created a nation reliant on cattle, sheep, and wheat. It is a rough country, sparse, drought prone and sunbaked, but Australia's pioneers, the ex-convicts and settlers who came as freemen, knew this great island had one thing Mother England and Europe didn't—space! It is space that allows the cattle and sheep to graze for miles on end. It is the picture of the leathery-skinned Aussie, sitting tall on a stock horse wearing his Akubra hat and oiled cotton raincoat, that remind us of the Old West. The **graziers** and **cow cockies** stand out as real today as they did a century ago. The work demands as much and never ends.

As for the time warp which makes parts of Australia feel 20 or 30 years behind the times, you can find it in the small country regional centers or shire seats. The low one- and two-story buildings shaded by overhanging roofs and quaint hotels with verandas all around hold back the hands of times. The dress is country casual, nothing trendy, just basic gear. The dusty boots and well worn brims tell the workmen's tale.

On the coasts, the endless summer continues. In the shadow of modern high rises or private mansions, or on the long stretches of open beach that circumnavigate the island, it is a modern scene. Hot trendy skimpy beachwear is the order of the day. Nothing prudish here. Tans are the only thing that cover most torsos. Surfing grabs most of the attention, but windsurfing, sailing, swimming, surf ski riding, belly boarding and anything else to do with water float right behind. Sydney may be the only city in the world where signs posted inside trains direct passengers not to put their surfboards on the seats!

Obviously, if you've read this far, you are one of those

many people ready to take a journey Down Under. One or all of these images draws you beyond the oceans and beyond the miles. If you prepare well for the possible pitfalls, the fun of the trek will travel with you as a close companion and stay with you as a special memory which will not fade.

Chapter 1

About Life Down Under

The Lucky Country has much about which to be boastful. An uncluttered life exists here. Closets do not need to be filled with heavy winter gear and houses open themselves to the outdoors easily. Verandas shade you from the noonday sun and tea breaks the day in quarters with an air of tradition that no boss could stare down. Australia is perhaps the world's most livable country. With all its positive qualities, it doesn't hold itself in such high esteem that you must live up to goals and agendas set by the rest of the world. Aussies live life on their own terms. No strong religion dominates here. No lore forces out-moded traditions on new generations. No airs and graces exist to stop people from being open and friendly.

Now that I have enticed you with these attractions of Australia and its residents, it is worth knowing a few facts about the island, its history, its place in the world.

In 1988, Australia celebrated its bicentennial. To some this was a strange date to choose. It was not the 200th anniversary of freedom, liberation or federation. It was not a date that marked Australia as a country. Instead it was the anniversary of the landing of the First Fleet in 1788—an event that established Australia as the world's largest penal colony, a dumping ground for the discards of British society as it was known in the

18th century. It began the genocide that almost wiped the aborigines off the face of the earth.

While this irony was not lost, it didn't stop the Aussies from rallying around the flag and showing a true spirit of patriotism and nationhood as was never seen before Down Under. The party went on for a year!

It wasn't until the turn of the 20th century that Australia became a nation of federated states governed by Parliament; but, it did not renounce its allegiance to the throne of England. The British monarch remained the sovereign of Australia, and the Union Jack remained prominent on the flag of the Southern Cross.

For generations, the language and culture have been based on Britain. But isolation, climate and the lack of established classes (as in Mother England) modified the British-ness of Australia somewhat. The face of the country began to change with immigration from Mediterranean countries after the two world wars. One of the largest Greek populations outside Greece resides in Australia and the second and third most-widely spoken languages are Greek and Italian.

Finally, in the 1970s, Australia changed its racist anti-non-white immigration policies. Asians and Blacks were allowed to settle within the confines of its shores, creating a new flood of immigration.

For the traveler, this new face of Australia adds a new dimension. Cities seem more cosmopolitan because of their diversity. Certainly there are more foods from which to choose. Conversations can be more lively and debate more frequent. Interest in the rest of the world has been heightened. Americans seem insular compared to Australians who fill their plates with a mix of world news, rather than only local. American newscasts, preoccupied with Washington and the hometown, do not offer as varied a fare as Australian television. Not that Australians are particularly well read, they just seem to get more of a cross section of news from overseas.

While you travel, you will come across Australians traveling as well. Recent years have brought a big push within the country for Aussies to spend their dollars at home. Of course, there will be plenty of Germans and Japanese as well, but Aussies on holidays can make great companions and be a wealth of information. They reckon the favor will be returned someday when they or their family cross your path again somewhere.

Stereotypes

Aussies do shy away from the stereotypical American though—the big Yank in an alligator shirt, plaid shorts or bright green trousers who speaks loudly enough for several floors of a hotel to hear him and who shouts alternately, "It's just like the States," and "We don't do it this way back home!" Get the picture?

Aussies have their stereotypes, too. "Norm" comes to

mind. He's a cartoon character but you'll find him on the streets, the beaches and in the pubs. He's the pot-bellied guy in the tank top and short shorts, wearing beach thongs and a grubby hat, who says, "'Oow-yer-goin'?" and isn't looking for an answer.

Aboriginal People

One group of people has been notably left out so far—the Aborigines. The relatively small population has been relegated to aboriginal reserves. Many others find themselves on the fringes of a society with which they can never truly identify. In the 1980s, civil rights groups began to pressure the government to return rights to tribal lands, among them one of Australia's greatest national attractions—Ayers Rock. "The Rock" in the red center of Australia is now referred to by its traditional name **Uluru**. It has been a place sacred to the aboriginal people since the **Dreamtime**, the time when the gods walked this earth, the time about which their creation myths were written. While the spectacle of Uluru remains accessible to the public, the local tribe has exercised its rights to declare certain areas too sacred for public display.

As Aborigines' rights move forward in people's minds, their arts and historic artifacts are becoming more protected and more sought after. This, too, is worth noting as you tour the country.

The Sun

Australia lives by the sun; and tellingly, it has one of the world's highest rates of skin cancer. So finally, warnings about the sun's damaging rays no longer go unheeded. That should hold for the traveler as well. A Cancer Society campaigns calls for everyone to "Slip. Slop. Slap." Translated it means: slip on a shirt; slop on the sunblock cream; and slap on a hat. That's fair warning. Children need special attention. The reflection off a surface can be as damaging as direct light from overhead. Kids should not be left uncovered. Think lightweight long pants and long-sleeved shirts and hats with big floppy brims or "Foreign Legion-style" flaps. If they need them in Africa, you'll need them in Australia. The sun is just as strong, even when the air is cool.

Chapter 2

Planning a Holiday

Everywhere I go people tell me they've always dreamed of going to Australia but few of them have ever done enough research to determine if they could make the trip. They seem overwhelmed with the thought of flying half-way around the world and back. It is a long way. Rule of thumb calls it 10,000 miles from New York, but think of the frequent flyer mileage you can pile up! The distance pays off with the wonders you will find at the other end.

First, try to secure a minimum of three weeks vacation. I recommend four or five but do not try to do it in less than three! Do not choose your time off until you have become acquainted with Australia and its seasons, so you can get the most out of your trip and the things you like to do.

Second, read through the following two sections: City-by-City and Month-to-Month. They note how the major cities fit into the puzzle map and explain the climate, annual events and other details to help you choose when you want to go.

If you are traveling with a young family, be sure to read the family notes in the general information of this book and special sections set aside to answer specifics about taking the **ankle biters** along (Chapter 4: Families Going Down Under, and Chapter 5: Family Touring).

Like everything else, it just takes helpful information and good planning.

For those interested in Aussie spectator sports, we note them in the City Sights section of Chapter 3. Water sports show up in The Beaches section. Other outdoor sports including skiing are found under Countryside Australia. Camping does not have a section of its own because Australia is a great camping country. Most state and national parks allow camping and almost every beach community has public and private campgrounds. Often they'll be advertized as **caravan parks**. **Caravans** are campers in tow which can be set up daily or semi-permanently. Some parks will rent on-site caravans per night as well as spaces to tent dwellers. **Combis** or **combi vans** are vans, usually Volkswagens, outfitted for eating and sleeping, which travelers can rent while touring.

Golf

Golf gets almost no mention in this book. The reason is simple. Australians love to play golf. So, it doesn't matter where you stay, you can always find a public golf course. With the exception of small beach resorts, no resort would be worth its salt if it didn't offer at least nine holes. Remember, golf takes space and that's one thing Oz does not lack. Wealthy Japanese have made Australia their weekend playground—mainly for golf!

Driving

If you plan to drive, remember Aussies drive on the opposite side of the road. Distances are measured in kilometers. The top legal speed in town is posted at 60km per hour (60km/h), about 35 mph. You can open up on highways aroun 100km/h (62 mph). So, drivers should consider every 100km as the equivalent of one hour on the roads—faster travel than back in the U.S.

Packing

How you pack depends on how you travel. If you like to go out in a dress or suit and tie regularly, then that is what you'll need. For the most part, however, Aussies only dress that way when they're working, and since you are on vacation, you have no reason to wear dress clothes. Before we had children, we would expect "jacket-and-tie-nights," events that demanded finer clothes—perhaps at a dressy restaurant which required a man to wear a tie. Now, with kids in tow, we are even more casual and have left those things home. We bring mostly "play" clothes: jeans, lightweight slacks, shorts (year-round up North), cotton sweaters, sneakers, sandals (or rubber thongs), t-shirts, a couple of swimsuits, maybe a sundress which doubles as a jumper for me and a lightweight blazer for my husband (just in case). In the heat of summer, you may want extra changes, but washing machines are easy to find. Backpackers obviously pack lighter than hotel travelers. Whatever you need for a week should take you through a longer trip. No one expects high fashion on holidays. Don't forget caps and wide-brimmed hats comfortable enough to wear all the time.

A good rule of thumb: **bring what you need**. While you may browse in trendy shops, unless you have a limitless budget, you'll find them far too expensive to buy the basics and you'll find a thin selection compared to the U.S. Even bring your own beach towel; they're not cheap in Oz. You may find a souvenir towel to bring home, but that may not be on day one.

Even toiletries run dear. You would be surprised how they can ruin a budget if you are not prepared. Include insect repellent and sunblock in your kit.

Inflight Bag

Because this is such a long trip, make sure your carry-on bag holds your basic toiletries, particularly moisturizers because the long flight can be very dehydrating. Lip moisture products, stick or cream, should be kept close by in a pocket or an easily accessible bag. You might find yourself reaching for it between drinks. A complete kit should contain: dental products, lip and skin care products, cosmetics or shaving gear, change of underwear, spare shirt (and slacks if possible), deodorant, chewing gum, lozenges or hard candies, reading material, puzzles or games, a cassette player with headphones, extra batteries and tapes.

The clothing changes help to make you feel fresh after a long night inflight or if your luggage is lost or delayed on the other end. And it's nice to have a clean change if a drink or food gets spilled on you (or if you, inadvertently in the dark, sit on a full plastic juice container!).

Also, bring a sports-style drink bottle which you can fill with ice and water or soft drink. Again this can help get through the long dry night when you may be too lazy/tired to get any liquid refreshment. Unlike a plastic cup, they can be tucked into a seat pocket when your tray is up (and it may keep you from hoarding those unopened plastic drink containers).

Inflight Bag Checklist

__ skin moisturizer
__ lip balm
__ toothbrush/paste
__ cosmetics/shaving gear
__ fresh underwear/plastic bag for laundry
__ spare shirt
__ deodorant
__ chewing gum/lozenges/hard candy
__ sports drink bottle
__ reading material/puzzles & games/pens
__ cassette player/headphones/books & music on tape/batteries

Month-by-Month

Organizing by Calendar and Climate

As a general note, remember the seasons are flip-flopped. Our winter equals their summer and vice versa. Events are listed here briefly for planning purposes. For more information check the appropriate section.

Summer Is December, January, February

December

Australians treat late December/January like Europeans treat August. If they can get away, they do. Kids begin a six-week school summer break and many people plan their family vacations at this time. If you are interested in an old-fashioned heavily ritualized Christmas, you will not find it in Oz. Some special events happen for Christmas but they more likely have to do with being at the beach or a barbecue. Poinsettias are in bloom as backyard bushes.

Airfares: Peak pricing starts December 1st and runs through January 31st.

Extremes: December through March marks "the Wet" season in the northern tropics, including Cairns, where it is an impossible time to travel.

Events: Sydney to Hobart Yacht Race begins Sydney Harbour on December 26th and finishes in Hobart, Tasmania. Activities on both ends are worth enjoying. Hobart Summer Festival underway.

January

School break ends around the end of January and the new school year begins. January 26th marks Australia Day. Like our July 4th, local events like carnivals or parades take place on the holiday itself or on a neighboring weekend. Australia, like the U.S., is not above creating long weekends out of traditional dates. In some states, the "holiday" may be altered year to year.

Events: Festival of Sydney; Tamworth's Country Music Festival (see Country NSW); Australian Tennis Open in Melbourne.

February

This is truly Australia's August, hot, and in many areas, humid (like Queensland). Extreme heat strikes the entire country, even if it's for only one week. Not a good month in which to travel if you can pick another.

Since the Aussies are used to their weather, summer's heat certainly doesn't stop the fun in seaside communities.

Airfares: February 1st through March 31st offer shoulder fares (mid-price).

Events: Festival of Perth (performing arts) gets underway and runs into March; Royal Canberra Show; Adelaide Festival (mixed arts) begins.

Autumn Is March, April, May

I choose March and April as favorite times to travel—except if you are committed to the Top End. Then it's still wet with monsoons and potential cyclones (hurricanes). However, you may find good weather in the lower Reef/Whitsunday Coast area. Leave that to the later part of your trip and enjoy the season's lower airfares.

March

Summer begins to wind down—the sun remains hot and the ocean is its warmest. But this is the beginning of autumn. Nights in the south begin to turn cool—a cotton **jumper** will do. Lovely traveling weather. Nothing extreme anywhere.

Events: Melbourne celebrates Moomba; Canberra Festival (arts); Perth Festival wraps.

Airfares: Still shoulder.

April and May

The moderate autumn weather continues. As of May, the dry season begins in the tropical North; but the box jellyfish prevent beach swimming, except in safety enclosures until June. Parts of New South Wales show off a kind of fall as does the city of Melbourne. Usually warm enough for outdoor swimming.

Airfares: April 1st marks the start of the lowest fare season. It continues through November. Check for special low rates earlier in the year for this time period. Sometimes they have to be purchased well in advance. (We missed by a week one year, loosing hundreds of dollars in savings for a family of four.)

Events: April has nothing annual or nationally noteworthy. In May is the Adelaide Cup (horse racing); Lions Fosters Camel Cup (camel races) in Alice Springs.

Winter Is June, July, August

June

June shepherds the change of season. Early winter begins to make minor alterations in the weather up north. Sydney and Perth continue to be pleasant and moderate. The chill begins to seep into Melbourne, Tasmania and cooler mountain and inland regions. Generally, still a pleasant time to travel, though southern beaches are chilly. Finally, you can swim off Far North beaches because box jellyfish season ends.

Events: none to mention.

July

The south starts feeling wintry. Melbourne dips no further than 40 degrees Fahrenheit and people don their homemade woolens. Queensland is like Florida in winter—pleasant but unpredictable. Sydney and Perth are mild.

Events: Cairns annual Agricultural Show; the Darwin Show.

August

Consider this month winter. Days are short. The Far North may be at its best for real adventurers. Nights in the desert can be cold for campers. Brisbane and the nearby coasts can be fickle, sunny enough for a beach picnic or wetsuit surfing one day and nasty damp and raining the next. Sydney can be rainy as well and Melbourne can be downright cold and dreary. If given the choice, forget August in Australia.

Extremes: Because most homes and other buildings have no central heat, you'll find the cold damp hard to escape (even in Queensland if you hit a rainy spell). You'll need to pack heavier socks and sweaters, sweat-suits for indoors/or sleeping, shoes and jackets to with-stand the wet. Campers should pack for cold nights.

Events: Darwin's Beer Can Regatta; Brisbane Show known as the Ekka.

Spring Is September, October, November

September

This month can still have a wintry holdover in the south, but elsewhere, by month's end, the days begin to warm and get longer. The doldrums start to end for Aussies. They look forward to their gardens and long days at the beach.

Events: The Melbourne Show; Footy Grand Final, Melbourne; Adelaide Show; Henley-on-Todd fake boat regatta in Alice Springs; Canberra's floral festival.

October

Spring truly begins. The North blooms. Purple jaca-randa trees color the treeline. West Australia's wild-flower season begins. Good time to travel.

Extremes: The box jellyfish are back along northern beaches for the rest of the year!

Events: Wildflower season, West Austalia.

November

While you may not think to take an extended vacation this late in the year...Do! November is wonderful Down Under. Not yet the searing heat of summer nor the Wet in the tropics (wait a month). Generally, warm enough to enjoy everywhere. Gardens and paddocks bloom and tulip time is underway in New South Wales and Victoria.

Airfares: Peak begins again December 1st, so take advantage.

Events: Melbourne Cup and Melbourne's Lygon St. Italian Festa; Formula One Grand Prix, Adelaide.

City-by-City

Queensland, the Sunshine State

Cairns

Cairns (pronounced *CANS*) is not a major population center but because Queensland is so large and the capital city so far south, Cairns has taken on a special persona. It has an international airport and thus is an international gateway to Australia as well as this tropical paradise. Cairns has become a popular starting point for adventure holidays because the Great Barrier Reef sits only 15 miles (24 km) offshore and tours of the rain forests and crocodile country of far north Queensland can be easily arranged.

Do not forget, Cairns is in the tropics and that means the dramatic weather the tropics offer. Summer is the beginning of the RAINY season, called simply, the Wet, which runs from December to April. Monsoonal downpours make travel difficult. But, remember, heat and humidity are the ingredients for a rain forest. The rest of the year is dry but very hot. The coast enjoys its breezes but the temperatures stay very high along with the humidity.

Note: if you think you will miss the Reef if you do not get to Cairns, think again. The Beaches section will explain all the jumping off points available further south along the Queensland coast.

Brisbane: Population 1.2 million

The state capital sits in the southeast corner of Queensland, only an hour inland from the beach playground known as the Gold Coast. Most trips to the region include a beach holiday as well as a city tour (but that can be said of a number of Aussie capitals).

On its own, Brisbane sports a lovely city center with colonial-style buildings and stately palm trees waving overhead. Once considered an out-of-the-way country

Planning a Holiday

city, Brisbane now hosts a fine downtown shopping area which moves at a pleasant pace, and first class hotels. The Brisbane riverfront has become trendy place for restaurants, cafes and boutiques.

Weather falls into the subtropical climate category. Not so distinctly wet and dry as further north. It's warm to hot year 'round. January can be too hot and muggy to handle while August at the other extreme can be damp, rainy and sometimes cooler than expected.

New South Wales, the Cradle of Australia

Sydney: Population 3.5 million

Australia's largest city. Sydney is best described as "stunning."

From the moment planes circle Botany Bay everyone is enthralled by the views of the big beautiful harbor and the familiar sight of the sail-like roofs of the Sydney Opera House.

Sydney began as the landing site for Australia's first penal colony in 1788. From there, a modern cosmopolitan city has evolved blessed with a beautiful climate and a dramatic natural setting.

The pace of life does not compare to slower Brisbane or proper Melbourne. It is casual but businesslike for the most part—tempered by a harbor and beaches that continually lure the population to come and play. As much as possible is done outdoors.

Water sports rate high on the agenda here and pleasant mountain retreats are accessible in about two hours by car, bus or rail.

The Australian Capital Territory (ACT)

Canberra: Population 300,000

Seat of the Federal Parliament. Canberra was a space carved out of the bush of New South Wales and designed on an empty canvas so that the ACT would forever stand alone, free of state rivalries. This uniquely planned city makes Canberra interesting (though critics say it is devoid of a human touch).

Parliament House and Old Parliament House explain the growth of the Australian nation. The city, being planned around a lake, offers a number of sports as well as serious sightseeing.

But, if you want to meet Aussies, Canberra is not the place. Diplomatic and government workers and news media make up most of the small ever-changing population.

Victoria, the Garden State

Melbourne: Population 2.9 million

The second largest city. Melbourne is as different from Sydney as Boston from Los Angeles. While Sydney glorifies in glitz, Melbourne has its grace.

Melbourne exudes a kind of colonial atmosphere, held over from the last century. The carefully placed State Parliaments Building leads the architectural way. Victorian cottages and terrace houses with their lace ironwork offers stark contrast to modern high rises. A central pedestrian mall with clanging trams acts as a wonderful reminder of another era.

The seasons change here, maybe not as dramatically as in New York, but they are evident. While summer can be hot (up to 100 or more degrees Fahrenheit), winter can dip into the 40s. Spring blooms in the Garden State and there are enough deciduous non-native trees in Melbourne to remind one of fall.

This is a big sports town—home of Australian Rules Football and the National Tennis Center.

South Australia: Study in Contrasts

Adelaide: Population one million

The state capital. If Melbourne wears the robes of the reliable sensible Queen of Australian cities, then Adelaide stands regally as her princess. Known as the "City of Churches," Adelaide has little in the way of skyscrapers to obstruct the views of spires gleaming in the sun.

Most tourists visit Adelaide as part of a wine country tour of South Australia. Racing car buffs have discovered the city, now home to the Australian Grand Prix—a formula one auto race.

The weather cooperates all year with a short wet season during the winter and temperatures ranging from 60-90 degrees.

Just beyond the comfortable part of South Australia, lies the Nullarbor Plain and the rest of the great desert.

Western Australia: The New Frontier

Perth: Population one million

If Australia is the world's closest thing to a mythical Land of Oz, then Perth may be deemed her Emerald City. Gleaming skyscrapers and pristine streets characterize Western Australia's solo city. Over 3,000 (4,800 km) miles of primarily desert land, not a yellow brick road, separate Perth from Sydney. New money, garnered from mineral mining, built this town and rebuilt the neighboring port as well. Most eastern Australians have never been to Perth, unless business or family has drawn them. Yachting and water sports enthusiasts might make the trip.

The Northern Territory: The Green and the Red

Darwin: Population 69,000

The Green Top End. Darwin serves as the gateway to Australia as the closest city to Asia. Many Americans would not know it exists except for World War II aficionados who know Darwin was bombed by the Japanese not long after Pearl Harbor.

Adventure travelers go to Darwin to start their tours of Kakadu National Park, a rain forest system and home to the wild regions captured in the movie *Crocodile Dundee*. From October to April, monsoons rage during the Wet. The opposite season, known as the Dry, encompasses the rest of the year. While it may not be rainy, it is still very humid and very hot. This is the real tropics and caution to deal with the sun, the heat and the **mozzies** should be taken.

Alice Springs: Population 20,000

While there is little in the way of a city or population here, "Alice," The Red Centre, marks a significant region in Australia. It remains the jumping off point for the deep dusty red heart of Australia, symbolized by Ayer's Rock (Uluru) and its stark surroundings. Pine Gap, situated just outside of town, serves as a U.S. military secret communications base.

Remember this is the desert—hotter than hot and drier than dry. But, even in the heat, there is a sense of humor. Every September, Alice hosts the annual Henley-on-Todd regatta—virtually an amusing foot race of fake boat costumes run in a dry creek bed, known as the Todd River. After heavy rains, the river does flood but that's uncommon enough for people to take pictures of it.

The Kangaroo Route (Getting There)

Once you resolve to go Down Under and have an idea of what you want to see and how to see it, it's time to look into getting there. Keep in mind this is not a short hop across the Atlantic. You want a well-organized plan. After all, if you have to be en route somewhere for more than 24 hours, you want the travel to go as close to plan as possible.

If your traveling party includes babies or children, read Chapter 4: Families Going Down Under, which details specifics that might affect your planning, in addition to this section.

First remember, all Americans need a passport and a visa. Visas are easy to obtain but you cannot get into the country without one. The Australian Tourist Commission can give you an application and other planning information (800-333-0199) or you can call the Australian Embassy in Washington or the Australian consulate in another part of the world. Offices are located in New York, Chicago, Los Angeles, Houston, Honolulu and Canada. (American tourists do not need visas for New Zealand.)

For most people, the Kangaroo Route is by air (unless you have some round-the-world plans which might take you cruising in the Pacific.) When looking into flights, have a long talk with your travel agent, going over all possible combinations of flights, time and connections. Keep good notes. Think about all of it before booking anything and always do it at least a month, if not two, before you plan to fly. That will allow you the most flexibility and chances at getting limited special rates. Several travel agencies deal specifically with Australian travel or Pacific travel. They can usually offer the best values and know how to organize the trip.

A Talk with a Travel Agent

Here are some tips for dealing with travel agents:

• Interview your agent: Has he/she made the trip to Australia before? (If you are planning for a family, find an agent who has made the trip with children of similar ages.)

• What are the best rates available in the coming months? Ask about specials. Explore fly\drive tours or packages about specific places you would like to see and things you would like to do.

• Are connecting flights to the West Coast included in the cost or discounted? What miles can be applied to frequent flyer programs? (Some international carriers work with some American programs. But in recent years, these deals have been known to change. Best not to assume anything.)

• Are all connections made through Los Angeles or are there other options? How much turn-around time is there in California?

(Too much is no good; less than two hours can mean a missed plane.)

• Are non-stop flights available from California to Sydney? If not, what stopovers are planned in the Pacific? Every stop lengthens your trip and adds potential problems.

• If you are not traveling on a package ask how many additional Australian cities are included in the airfare? What discounts are available for air travel within Australia?

• Can I book car rentals in advance?

Major carriers with routes from North America to Australia include the following: Qantas, Air New Zealand and United.

The airline you choose may depend on the time you would like to leave from the U.S. and from which California city, how long you can stand being in transit, the time of year, whether you are traveling with an infant and whether you collect frequent flyer miles.

When speaking with the travel agent, several points should be kept in mind. You want to speak to someone who is an experienced long-distance traveler. Empathy encourages good service. If you're traveling with little children or older people who need special services, try to find an agent who has experience.

If you are happy to make Sydney your first port of call in Oz, try to book a non-stop from Los Angeles. Several carriers offer non-stops. The 12 to 14 hours over the Pacific may seem like an eternity, but one long flight makes the entire trip more efficient. The long night in the air gets broken up by a couple of movies and leaves lots of time to sleep.

The alternative remains landing on a Pacific island. For example: You can de-plane at Honolulu at 1a.m. and spend two hours or so in a virtually closed terminal in the middle of the night. No comfortable lounges, just a rowdy waiting area. Families with little ones may find this a welcome break but more about those pros and cons in the family section.

By rule of thumb, most people say the trip takes 24 hours from New York and about 18 from California (12-14 non-stop); but, be prepared for up to 30 hours in transit or even more if you experience a big delay. (I've had one so-called "direct" trip take over 40 hours!)

If Sydney does not rank first on your itinerary, ask about direct (not non-stop) flights to other cities. If the Great Barrier Reef beckons, you may want to fly straight to Cairns and plan the rest of your trip from there. Or, with weather in mind, you may want to start your trip in Melbourne and head north.

A few words of caution: if, after doing all your research, you plan to travel during the southern winter, do not accept a flight that makes a layover in New Zealand (unless that is your primary destination). What is billed as a short stopover can turn into hours of wasted time. New Zealand can get very foggy in winter and cause flights to be rerouted. You could wind up landing on a different Pacific Island altogether and be forced to sit and wait until your initial port is clear. The potential delays become innumerable. (Personally, I've had this happen both times I flew through New Zealand in winter and will never allow it to happen again. Once I had a seven-hour delay and another time it meant three hours seated on a plane on the ground in Fiji with a fidgety two year old.)

Seasons and Fares

The travel year is broken into three seasons: Peak, Shoulder and Basic.

Peak—December 1st through January 31st/high summer.

Shoulder—February 1st through March 31st/summer, early autumn.

Basic—April 1st through November 30th/autumn, winter, spring.

Roundtrip coach or economy tickets can range from $900 to $1,500 depending on season, booked 21 days in advance.

Business class, which offers a few creature comforts, will cost about $4,600 round trip!

First class is reserved for the truly wealthy reaching over $7,000 round trip. Rarely do those ticket prices change according to season.

Connections

Make sure you have enough turn-around time in California because flights to Australia only leave once a day, at most. If missed, you'll have a 24-hour stay in California, costing you time and the expense of rearranging your plans. I suggest two to three scheduled hours because it's easy for flight delays to eat into that, especially if you are routed through a hub airport before getting to California.

You will find one other minor inconvenience flying Qantas and Air New Zealand because they are international carriers. If you arrive in Los Angeles by air, you will have to switch from the domestic terminal to the international terminal to catch your next flight or vice versa. While you may be fresh enough on the trip out not to be bothered by this, you may find it uncomfortable on the return after your long trip across the Pacific. Of course, your baggage will be interlined but the rest of your gear must go with you. In winter, you may want to keep a jacket for this jaunt outside following your airline representative from terminal to terminal. (More in Chapter 4)

A Note about Stopovers in Sydney

If your first destination is not Sydney, you may have to go through Sydney anyway to change planes for your final stop. It's a hike to the international transit area, which services flights from Asia and the Pacific as well as the Americas. The Sydney transit area is rather unpleasant, rather like a big hallway and a typical seating area. The restrooms are not spacious either. Qantas, however, has created a special transit lounge for its passengers, offering complimentary hot and cold soft drinks and snacks, television and restrooms. The wall of windows looks over active gateways (giving you something at which to stare for a while).

Some flights will fly directly into Melbourne, Brisbane or Cairns. None are non-stop. Usually you change planes in Hawaii. Choose whether you would like your layover in the middle of the trip in the middle of the night in Hawaii or at the end of the trip in Sydney. But, try not to get stuck with both on the same flight! It will be a long trip.

The Airlines to Oz

Armed with all this information, let's take a look at the five major carriers which service the Pacific route.

Qantas

Qantas is the official airline of Australia. Tails on Qantas jets sport a kangaroo and the airline ambassador is a koala. As an airline, Qantas is impressive—having the finest safety record of worldwide carriers and boasts one of the youngest fleets in the air. Qantas flies in Australia on a limited basis—only between international ports. A ticket may allow one or two additional stops inside Australia, but your choice of flights will be minimal. However, that option is a money saver and it allows you to leave the country from a different city than the one in which you landed. Other locations must be serviced by domestic airlines (ask your travel agent to help you work out your itinerary. It will save money.)

Generally, Qantas service ranks very high. Crew members are helpful and courteous. They immediately greet you with the expected **G'day**! Stewardesses are referred to as **hosties**, short for air hostesses. Stewards remain stewards. Spacewise, we've noticed a consolidation on newer planes, making the seating a little more crowded, but no less than on U.S. carriers. The crew stocks the bar with an assortment of Australian wine and beer and the food selections often have an Australian character about them. The choices, including fresh tropical fruits in season and children's meals, are usually quite good, not the bad T.V. dinner stuff served by some carriers.

On the ground, the Sydney transit lounge adds comfort to the trip.

Qantas makes a point of helping families with special services, noted in the family section.

Qantas is often the highest fare but sometimes they

join the fare wars during off seasons and have been very competitive. After flying with several of the carriers over a number of years, I am the most confident with Qantas, even if the ticket costs an extra hundred dollars.

Air New Zealand

Air New Zealand offers competitive rates and is often cheaper than Qantas but they must land in New Zealand before going to Australia. That can add hours to the trip (and as we said earlier, can be a real problem during their winter). If New Zealand is part of your itinerary, then certainly consider Air New Zealand. Kiwi service is good generally but delays may not be handled as well as you like in New Zealand itself, if you are unlucky enough to get stuck in an airport there.

If for some reason you are bent on booking with Air New Zealand, you may be able to tie in with Qantas and take a non-stop across the Pacific. This is part of a marketing agreement between the two airlines, which allows a limited number of passengers to cross over. In the end, your ticket will say Air New Zealand but you will be on a Qantas plane! This service helps if you are including time in kiwi country, but would like non-stop service in one direction.

U.S. Pacific Route Carriers

At one time, there were three carriers to Australia. By mid-1994, only one still flew Down Under. Of course, that could still change if an airline again bids on the Pacific route. *Always* ask your agent for the latest details.

United

United offers the economy passenger domestic-style travel on an overseas flight. Even the newest planes do not accommodate families especially well (see family section). If your trip does not originate in Los Angeles, beware. Because United flies all over America you can get stuck with some complicated domestic routing that can really add time to a trip. Make sure the agent is aware of every stopover and options. Because we often have a narrow time slot in which to travel we have been burned with terrible routing. If you have the luxury of good planning, start here. Many United flights pass through New Zealand. Caution noted earlier.

Adding the Miles

For some travelers, frequent flyer programs can tip the balance when choosing an airline to fly. This trip gives you good reason to consider that decision. After all, more than 20,000 miles are at stake when you fly half way around the world and back.

Obviously, United counts all miles racked up on their flights, but keep in mind both Qantas and Air New Zealand have partnership deals with U.S. carriers.

In 1994, Qantas continued its relationship with American Airlines. The entire trip is counted toward future travel. (When American also flew to Australia, they did not accept Qantas miles which upset the plans of frequent Qantas flyers. However, with American no longer touching down Down Under, the program has been reinstated.)

Air New Zealand has a similar partnership with Delta Airlines. So the choice is yours, depending on your domestic preference.

Chapter 3

Focusing Your Trip

While making your decisions about Australia, think of the kinds of things you would like to do while Down Under. If you feel like a typical tourist, you may want to find a package tour that suits your fancy. An atypical tourist may want to indulge his personal interests and select tour sites accordingly.

In Australia, you can focus your trip either on the things the landscape and seascape offer or the ways you like to travel (camping vs. hotels) and the priorities you have set for things to see and do. The following will not be an in-depth look at the choices but rather a menu to whet your appetite.

Once you have a good idea, the Australian Tourist Commission (with offices in major cities in the United States and toll-free number 800-333-0199) and State Tourist offices (some of which have offices in North America) can help you with specifics. Once in Australia, the state offices or the Royal Automobile Club (like the AAA here) of each state will be glad to offer local information that can change from month to month or year to year. The Royal Automobile Club is referred to by its acronym **RAC**, with the state letter added on. Example: **RACQ** covers Queensland and the **RACV** covers Victoria. As long as it's RAC, it's all the same.

Almost every **shopping centre** (meaning local village

or shopping area) houses an information center which will feature information regarding smaller tourist attractions, fun parks, outdoor sports and rental equipment.

Clean and safe **ablution blocks** or public bathrooms exist along the roadsides, in parks and near most main beaches. Councils maintain them better than you might imagine and for a country that lives outdoors, they take pride in their cleanliness and availability. Most large parks have public barbecue areas and some councils stock them with wood for your convenience; others offer gas grills. Just bring your **esky** and the **barby** is on.

As this section refers to city areas, you might find it helpful to refer back to the City-by-City guide for more information.

The Beaches, the Barrier Reef and Water Sports

Being an island, Australia will never be short of beaches and hopefully they will remain as picturesque and pristine (for the most part) as they appear today. Every state slips into the sea at some point. Not all beach areas fit the same description.

Tropical beaches can be hot and glorious one time of year and drenched by the rainy season the other half of the year. If the rains do not trouble you, the remoteness, the sharks and the lethal box jellyfish might. Some beaches sport bigger surf than others; many have waves more conducive for family play. The ocean is warmer in the north than the south, some beaches don rocky facades, others cloak themselves in fine, almost talc-like sand. Ah! the choices to keep in mind when selecting a beach holiday!

No one can own the foreshore in Australia. Private beaches, like beach clubs, etc., do not and cannot exist by law. Beaches are free and unrestricted. Public access must be guaranteed at certain reasonable intervals (determined by law), even in sections where beach-side building has been allowed or where large private properties, like estates and farms, might block access from the roadside.

Swimming safely means swimming on a posted beach where **surf lifesavers** select the safest swimming area and post flags for boundaries. Undertows pose dangers as do other marine threats. Councils set up shark nets and jellyfish enclosures to protect some beach areas as well, particularly in the tropical north. For families, especially, safety should be the first consideration.

If your trip does not include long drives, then any of these areas may be reached by flying in and out of local airports or taking busses (though the distances by bus can seem magnified). Again check with local agencies which can pin down the regularity of flights and ways of getting to and from airstrips.

As far as these notes are concerned, the beach communities listed are good picks for travelers but there is no way that every beach and beach town can be listed. Highlights will include places to surf, dive, snorkel, deep sea fish, boat and tour—and all the wonderful water sports in between. If you choose to circumnavigate Australia by car and have months to do so, you will probably find some little jewels that only locals enjoy. Savor them and make them your secret. For now, we'll just look at the more accessible parts of this coastal paradise.

One other perquisite of beach hopping in Australia—the food! Local seafood, from the unusual **bug** to the world's largest **crayfish** (lobsters) and unique reef fish like coral trout and other specialties, including barramundi and John Dory, will stir your appetite and give you another good reason not to leave.

Enough generalities and words of caution! Let's go around the country:

Queensland Beaches

The Tropical North

No winter here; the weather stays hot year-round. But the summer rainy season, known simply at **the Wet,** runs from December to April and ocean swimming is prohibited because of the **stingers**, the lethal box jellyfish or sea wasp, that spawn in the summer along the mainland. Stingers do not inhabit the reef or island waters. Some communities have beach enclosures which allow safe swimming. Otherwise, they prohibit swimming because one sting from a transparent tentacle can be deadly. Divers can wear **stinger suits** or common panty hose for protection. (Aussie men in pantyhose?)

Once a tropical fishing village, **Cairns,** in the last decade, has grown into a booming regional center, with an international airport, resorts and other accommodations that offer access to marvelous beaches and the Great Barrier Reef, only 15 miles (24 km) offshore. Further down the coast, similar sandy beaches offer pockets of places to stay. Local beach towns serve the neighboring farm communities where the staples of sugar cane, pineapples and bananas grow in abundance.

The Barrier Reef

The Reef stretches 1,250 (3,000 km) miles along the Queensland coast and is divided into several sections and entry points. The Reef itself comes under the authority of the **Great Barrier Reef Marine Park**, an Australian government operation. Expensive island resorts lay short distances offshore, a few are true coral keys on the outer reef but most are land formations detached from the mainland. Any travel agent can tell you about the 20 or so developed islands, but you can choose from many economical ways to enjoy the area as well.

Colorful Coral

The abundance of sea life, the size and scope of the coral beds and the intensity of color should not be missed by anyone who has come this close. Look but don't touch unless a guide says you can. Some beauties are really **nasties**, things that might hurt.

For the casual tourist not strictly on a diving vacation, boat tripping and reef walking tours invite them to explore a piece of this wonder. You don't have to be named Cousteau to find it brilliant and fascinating. Of course, one quick visit may hook you into becoming adventurous enough to squeeze into a wet suit, but you don't have to deep-sea dive to get a feeling for nature's marine marvels.

Divers' Paradise

For scuba divers from around the world, the Reef is **The Reef**. No other undersea park is larger than this. Points of entry are innumerable: as close as a few miles offshore in the far north to a plane ride away further down the Queensland Coast. Every resort community has a dive shop with experienced divers who can offer tours and information about diving. American equipment interchanges easily with Aussie gear and diving regulations appear less strict than in the U.S. Even if you've never worn diving gear, but the Reef lures you to try, most hotels and dive shops can arrange lessons and packages to get you out there for a day or a week. **Cairns** probably has the largest selection of dive packages and some say the least expensive compared to other jumping off points.

Fisherman's Treat

Over 1,500 species of fish inhabit the reef with many edible sport fish among them. The ribbon reef stretching 180 miles (308 km) north from Cairns, home to the giant black marlin, draws sport anglers from all over the world.

The Whitsunday Coast and Islands

Whitsunday is barrier reef country at its best. The little town of **Airlie Beach** and its neighbor **Shute Harbour** are the central land points. Airlie has the accommodations and the restaurants along its little main street and Shute Harbour has the seaplanes and every kind of marine craft available, from little skiffs to big party boats, sailing cruisers and deep-sea fishing boats. Flights from Brisbane and Cairns land at **Proserpine** Airport, the nearby country city that serves as the regional center. (Propserpine is worth a look. Its main street has not changed since the fifties and that makes it very quaint.)

For divers, Airlie offers great access to the reef; it's

closer to Brisbane and the rest of Queensland and has a charm unmatched by other places along the coast. For swimming, Airlie has a protected enclosure because it is the southernmost part of stinger country. All levels of accommodations are available from campsites to luxury hotels looking down from the hills. This area bears the reputation as the cruising capital of Australia. Bareboat tours and charter rentals can take you cruising for days around the 74 islands and hundreds of protected anchorages.

Highlight

Pick a day cruise and slowly slip over the warm clear blue water, snorkeling around a fringe coral bed; then take an hour or two to visit an island beach. Or you can organize a seaplane tour over the incredible sight that is the expansive reef; or fly to an anchored boat/resort or an island resort if time or money allow. The cruise and the aerial view of the reef will leave indelible impressions.

Sunshine Coast

If by a beach holiday, you mean a little sun, a little surf, a little golf, a little sightseeing, leisurely meals and various family entertainment, this area serves one of the best combinations. From Noosa Shire down through Maroochy Shire are the most inviting beaches; beautiful sunny days beckon you throughout the year. This somewhat rural coast offers a pleasant selection of beach towns from the international resort of **Noosa Heads** with its big-name hotels, boutique shopping and fine dining to the more casual surfside village of **Coolum Beach** (where there will never be more than the existing two high-rises) or the river's mouth regional center of **Maroochydore**. They offer a wide range of playtime in the sand and surf. Accommodations range from rented **caravans** (campers) to luxury resorts. Motels and rental units fill the middle ground.

Also at Noosa, **Noosa National Park** encompasses rain forests which reach down the mountain toward the powdery white beaches, enjoyed by surfers and bathers. Surfers or **boardies** go to Noosa for the long wave. They may not be the world's largest waves, but catch them right and they run for a long time.

Families will find hospitable playing spots in the still waters of the many creeks which feed the Pacific—local residents can tell you where they hide. Family-style tourist attractions abound along the coast and in the Hinterland. Again information centers can be found in every shopping center here as elsewhere in Oz, so take advantage. The possibilities range from horseback riding to mini-golf, riverboat rides to **Underwater World**, an oceanarium at **Mooloolaba**. (See family section for more highlights.)

The **Wharf at Mooloolaba**, a recent development which includes the spectacular Underwater World Oceanarium, offers alternatives to the beach—fishing boats, boat tours and a good dive shop can certainly help fill a visit there (not to mention some nice restaurants, boutiques and a great playground).

Maroochydore, at the mouth of the Maroochy River, offers similar alternatives, but add good windsurfing or sailboarding, waterskiing and catamaraning on the river to the list. Swimming and picnicking are also possible. For a more leisurely day trip, perhaps when the weather stays cool, take a paddlesteamer on a history tour up river past the sugar cane plantations that first brought settlers and prosperity to the area.

The Sunshine Coast can be reached easily by car from Brisbane. The southern town of **Caloundra** is just an hour's drive and Noosa is only two hours away. Airlines and busses service the area, too.

The Gold Coast

If you were to drive south along the coast, long before

you arrive at the Gold Coast you would spot the city of **Surfers' Paradise** (called **Surfers**), standing like Miami Beach. While the surf may have been the original draw to this part of Queensland, glitz and kitsch now outweigh the simpler beach culture. High-rise units and hotels overshadow the beach so sunset comes early in certain sections. However, the buildings were never constructed on the foreshore, so clear views of the parks, dunes and beaches from the roadside and **footpath** (sidewalk) remain.

If your idea of a beach holiday includes real surfing on big waves, great sun and warm water by day; and casino gambling, dining and dancing by night, Surfers and surrounds sounds like your kind of vacation resort. Label this area Brisbane's playground since it's only an hour drive away (a little more in heavy weekend traffic).

One recent criticism of Surfers: because it has become a big draw for Japanese tourists, even the Aussie souvenir stores, which sell opals, koala-everything and sheepskins, appear to be owned and operated by Japanese. This detracts from the feeling of being in Australia and the opportunity to commune with local shop owners about their way of life.

The northern Gold Coast begins at **Southport** just above Surfers. Marinas there provide a good variety of marine craft and tours. The Gold Coast continues south the length of southern Queensland to the New South Wales border at **Coolangatta**. While not as **flash** (ostentatious or fancy) as Surfers, Coolangatta boasts terrific surfing and famous **surf carnivals** where beach-sport freaks from all over Australia compete for medals in such competitions as **Iron Man**, a beach triathalon, surf-ski racing and team lifesaving. The carnivals bring the whole place alive. Carnivals can be found in other beach towns as well. For the tourist, they create a colorful sight and a unique peek at Aussie culture.

In between the two main towns, lies an unending

string of smaller ones along the Pacific Highway or Route One. Suburban sprawl took over a long time ago and, unless you're paying attention, you may have a hard time remembering whether you have come to Australia or stayed in Florida. (Watch out! One town stole the name Miami!) American food chains abound. But walk the few blocks from the highway to the beach and you know this cannot be America. To stand on **Mermaid Beach** and stare down the 15-mile uninterrupted sweep to Coolangatta or look the other way north to Surfers leaves you in awe of the size of this land and the freedom existing along the coast. Motels offer even the last-minute visitor plenty of accommodations, some with efficiency kitchens.

For additional shopping off the main drag, but reachable by bus, is Pacific Fair Mall, a huge shopping complex with typical mall-style stores, trendy t-shirt shops, diving gear and Aussie souvenirs. The great palm trees and outdoor eating courts keep you from feeling like you're in the Midwest but beyond that a mall is a mall.

New South Wales Beaches

The North Coast

From the border town of **Tweed Heads**, where the Tweed River meets the ocean, the Pacific Highway meanders toward and away from the coast. For miles, small beach communities, not as geared for international tourism as their neighbor, the Gold Coast, dot the oceanside. The weather becomes more temperate as you go further south and every beach is inviting.

Coffs Harbour seems to be the main selection for this area above Sydney. For southern Australians, Coffs seems to be the holiday choice for those who don't want to go as far north as Queensland. A pretty area with

©1993

nontropical weather, it becomes a draw when Queensland is too humid or too wet.

Ask about whale watching in this area in the winter. Humpbacks can be seen off the **Cape Byron Lighthouse** from June through September.

Port Macquarie sits farther south on the coast. Another booming area, the town offers lovely beaches and enough accommodation for the traveler. As a port, it provides boaters and fishing enthusiasts with plenty of distractions.

Sydney

Perhaps because Sydneysiders love the water, their beaches are known around the world. They may not be as sweeping as those in other parts of Australia, but being only a train ride away makes them easily accessed by this cosmopolitan city. **Bondi** (pronounced *Bond-eye*) holds the blue ribbon. Surfers, topless bathers, the avant-garde, the tourist and the family all flock here. In some ways, Bondi defines Aussie beach culture, the way Malibu does (or did) in California. If it's popular at Bondi, it must be the thing to do. **Takeaway** shops line one edge and apartment buildings overlook the other. Many **Sydneysiders** head across **Sydney Harbour** to **Manly**, another lovely beach community which services locals and tourists.

The South Coast

Below Sydney, within a day's drive is **Kiama**, another good beach selection and even further south, heading toward the Victorian border, lie **Bateman's Bay**, **Bega** and **Eden**, all resort towns that make good stopovers if you're auto-touring in this region. Many of them have reputations for fishing and boating, as well as good seafood prepared from local catches. This area marks the end of the South Pacific Coast.

Victoria's Beaches

Southeast Victoria

Leaving New South Wales, the coast curves under Australia and is bounded by the Tasman Sea. The **Croajingolong National Park** takes in the first section of coast and provides beautiful beaches, park services and a scenic lighthouse area. Victorians enjoy the inlet town of **Mallacoota**. While inside the park, it offers accommodations and food services. Continuing southwesterly along Route One, or the Princes Highway as it's called at this point, you will come to **Lakes Entrance**, a vacation town, known for boating and other water sports. The region is called the **Gippsland Lakes**, the collection of lakes just behind **Ninety Mile Beach**, a barrier island. The Lakes host power boating, windsurfing and waterskiing enthusiasts, as well as fishermen and families just looking for a lovely holiday.

The water from the Southern Ocean is colder than in the Pacific and it feeds this area. This entire region is called Gippsland and is Victoria's farmbelt. The locals take advantage of all the beaches and the great fishing and boating they offer.

Wilson's Promontory

The next most prominent point along the way aptly bears the nickname the **Prom**. A hilly, rocky peninsula that once was the geographic link between the mainland and Tasmania, now **Wilson's Promontory National Park** acts as an outdoor retreat. Beautiful bays and beaches for leisure along with nature walks over hill and dale and through bird sanctuaries offer nice contrast for a beach holiday. The Prom boasts one of Australia's largest campgrounds; and rental lodges and apartments are available. Remember, this area does get winter—a rainy dreary time that is more like an Northern American autumn. So this is no place for a beach vacation then. During the summer and school holidays, the Prom provides a near-home getaway for Victorians, so its best to check availability of accommodations either by calling the National Park office or the RACV.

Port Phillip Bay

Think of Port Phillip Bay in the shape of a man with arms held out as if holding a large basket, the hands and fingers pointing inward. **Melbourne** replaces the head. From there on both sides the coast provides the shoulders, arms and hands. On the eastern side, down the Nepean Highway, the flattened hand becomes the **Mornington Peninsula**. The towns of **Rosebud**, **Sorrento**, **Portsea** and **Rye** attract tourists from all over. Steeped in history, they provide both bayside and surf beaches, offering families a choice. Windsurfing and catamaraning from the beaches present alternatives for busy days in the sun.

Melbourne

Melbourne has city beaches and suburban beaches, marinas and lots of beachside parkland. But these are not the beaches Australia is known for. They do not have waves. They are bay beaches, splash-in-the-water beaches. That's true for the rest of the way west down the other arm and finally back to the coast of **Bass Strait**, the ocean waterway dividing Tasmania and Victoria.

The Great Ocean Road

This winding road clings to the coast providing breathtaking views and access to beach towns for over 80 (128 km) miles along this battered and beaten shoreline.

With the battering and the beating from the winds and waves of the Southern Ocean comes a surfers' Shangri-la, where international surfing championships take place. The winter waves at **Torquay** and **Bells Beach** rise 10 to 15 feet out of the ocean. While Torquay has places for swimming and good accommodations, Bells stands alone as a surfers' haven, too deep and too rough for anything else. The next towns of note for surfing and swimming include **Lorne** and **Apollo Bay**.

Port Campbell National Park

The dramatic coastline for which the Great Ocean Road became famous begins at Princetown and continues for 20 miles (32 km) west. The Port Campbell National Park encompasses the shoreline along the road, a rough terrain that looks down on the **Twelve Apostles**—great monoliths carved by the sea and standing like men in the water. While they are probably the most breathtaking, the **Arch** and **London Bridge,** both carved by nature from stone, fascinate onlookers equally. Paths wind down to the rocky sandy edge and tell tales of famous shipwrecks and other disasters. A gray winter sky makes the coast daunting and turns the Apostles into ghost-like forms; meanwhile, the summer sun renders the rock formations playful and charismatic.

In winter, Southern Right whales can be "watched" off the coast.

The rest of the Victorian coast offers beach areas, parkland and fishing spots. Some historic communities which started as whaling centers will be mentioned in other sections.

South Australian Beaches

While still heading west, the coastline turns north into the **Great Australian Bight**. Large peninsulas jut into the Bight creating more than one gulf with waves less ferocious than those directly on the Southern Ocean. There are national park barrier beaches and other harbor and beach towns to choose from.

Adelaide and Surrounds

From **North Haven** to **Brighton**, Adelaide's coast forms one long calm surf-less beach. In summer, the beaches, popular with the locals, can be enjoyed by tourists, too.

For a day trip that will bring you to fine beaches, ferry rides, wineries, etc., travel due south of Adelaide for a half hour or so and peruse the **Fleurieu Peninsula**. Its farthest tip, **Cape Jervis**, looks toward **Kangaroo Island.** The island's main town of **Kingscote** can be reached by ferry. Travelers say Kangaroo Island makes a great stopover for deep-sea fishing, swimming and taking in the native wildlife, especially at the western end of the island in **Flinders Chase National Park.** Though not a coral reef, diving is popular in this area. Again check local dive shops for information.

Two more peninsulas make up this part of the coastline: **Yorke Peninsula** and the **Eyre Peninsula.** Both offer similar variety and attractions. Small historic points dot the areas too, since these are some of Australia's earliest settlements.

Western Australia's Beaches

Western Australia, like Queensland, has endless miles of coastline; much of it is somewhat inaccessible, not near major cities or resorts and the top end is extremely hot. Divers touring Western Australia will have a chance to find venues in the Southern Ocean as well as the Indian Ocean.

The South Coast

If you are driving from South Australia, following Route One, you will cross the **Nullarbor Plain** at the top end of the Bight and cross the border into Western Australia. Past the Plain the highway will turn south again toward the coast and meet the water at a town called **Esperance,** located amid brilliant blue waters, snow white beaches and little islands. One of the attractions here is the twilight beach scenic loop drive.

This is the beginning of the populated bottom triangle

of West Australia (no density, just more population than elsewhere in the state). The first major town west of Esperance is **Albany**, located on the southernmost tip of Western Oz. This former whaling town was berth for the whalers who fended off the Southern Ocean and took their catch. It's still a great place for whale watching, and modern day fishing enthusiasts can enjoy themselves as well.

Further west the smaller towns of **Denmark**, **Northcliffe** and **Augusta,** still over 200 miles (320 km) south of Perth, provide ideal sites for camping, boating, fishing and, of course, ocean swimming. Sensational views go hand in hand with the southern coast.

The next section of the Indian Ocean is considered the **Margaret River Coastline**, home to some of the continent's most thrilling year-round surfing, windsurfing in the waves and other water sports. Small bays, like **Geographe Bay**, make diving in coastal waters a treat and many of the coves and bays along the coast provide surf-free bathing and calm waters for other sporting enthusiasts. Look for **Cape Naturaliste** and **Cape Leeuwin** for some of the world's finest big wave surfing.

Perth

While Perth is not an ocean port, it is situated on the beautiful Swan River, 15 miles (24 km) from the mouth at **Fremantle**. The Swan provides beautiful safe havens for water craft of all sizes. Sailboarding and waterskiing can be done in view of the city skyscrapers. Fremantle, home to the only America's Cup races held outside America to date, is a yachtsman's dream. If you fly into Perth, your feet can take you everywhere and quick bus service carry you to **Free-oh** as well. The long stretches of suburban beaches are incredibly beautiful in the morning, but when the Doctor blows (that's the cooling afternoon wind off the ocean) they can be a bit too blustery for sunbathing. The surfers love it then.

North Coast

Most people do not look for beach holidays up this way because it is so far from everywhere. However, there are two beach communities up north that might be worth the stop. **Geraldton**, 200 miles (320 km) north of Perth, wears the moniker "The Rock Lobster Capital of the World." That means great eating, but also good boating and sport fishing. Another thousand miles (1,600 km) along the coast, you come to **Broome**, the "Pearling Capital" of Australia. Culturally, Broome is a mixed bag because of its pearl diving history. Settlers from Japan, Singapore and Malaysia brought with them their food and festivals, all of which remain part of the Broome scene, along with a good sandy beach and diving.

The Top End

Most of the Top End in the **Northern Territory** is adventure and four-wheel drive country, noted in the Outback and Rain Forests section. But, if you've gone to the top to visit the city of Darwin, it has city beaches to enjoy but this *is* the tropics—the wet season and the jellyfish problems mirror those in Queensland.

Tasmania's Beaches

Tasmania, the island state of this island nation, sits below Victoria in the Southern Ocean. While not an Australian hot spot, beaches in little coves and bays throughout the island make for beautiful days in the summer sun. To get the most out of the waters of Bass Strait take the 14-hour ferry ride from Melbourne to the north coast town of **Devonport**. Do not tour **Tassie** without your **cozzie**. Tassie's east coast towns of **St. Helen's** and **Scamander** offer opportunities for fishing, skin diving and surfing. Fishing and diving gear can be rented in the "big" cities of **Hobart** and **Launceston**.

The Outback

Back of Bourke or **Back of Beyond** and **Beyond the Black Stump** represent a small part of the long list of phrases Aussies use to describe the **Never Never**—the land called the **Outback**. The mountains of the **Great Dividing Range** keep the east coast separated from the continent, which blocked early western settlement. The land beyond was the Outback and that has never changed. Australia's population lives on the narrow fringe. Everything else is Outback.

The Outback is mostly uninhabitable desert and at best uninviting, however fascinating. Aborigines of Australia roamed the Outback as nomadic tribes. Today their tribal homelands are being returned to them but it is mostly land that whites never wanted except to ogle. The Outback's sparse plains take four acres to feed one head of cattle. It is cattle **stations** the size of Montana or it is the **Nullarbor Plain**. While many people think all Australia is Outback, most Aussies have never spent more than a short time Outback if at all.

The Centre

In the dusty heart of Australia, in the lower portion of the **Northern Territory**, there is the place called the **Red Centre**.

Uluru

Within the Centre exists a magical place, spiritual ground to the Aborigines and awesome to the traveler. **Ayers' Rock**, the world's largest monolith, will take your breath away: first by the sight of its changing colors and then at the sheer magnitude of the hike. Like the Grand Canyon in Arizona, once you are there, you feel you must tread on its paths, feels its sand and stone beneath your feet, experience the exhilaration of completing the trek. Then you know why the aboriginals worshiped here and fought to be able to call the land their own and hear modern Australians call it **Uluru**—not owned by the white man—but by the spirits of the earth.

Most travelers come to Uluru via **Alice Springs**, the heart of the Northern Territory. (A 20-hour ride from Adelaide is an alternative.) Uluru is a five-hour drive, 250 miles (435 km) southwest of the city. You can get there by car or bus trip through the dramatic landscape to a place called **Yulara**. **The Yulara Resort** complex was commissioned by the government in 1984 to create a place for tourists to stay while visiting **Uluru** and **Kata Tjuta** (known as the Olgas), the surrounding giants'-head-like monoliths. The self-sufficient village was built to blend with the scenery and prevent ugly sprawl on roadways nearby. All levels of accommodation have been made available at different price ranges.

The land was returned in name to the Aborigines in 1985, who in turn leased it back to the National Park Service. Rental cars are available and so are bus tours of the Rock, 12 miles (20 km) from the resort. At sunrise and sunset, the great rock runs through its colorful changes. Like a painter adding layers to a canvas, the sun changes the rock from orange to red to deep purples and back to her natural red again. Viewing areas are clearly marked and shutterbugs jostle for position.

Outdoors in the Outback must be revered. This is a harsh land. The windy top of the rock can be 110 degrees in the summer. It is a steep one-mile climb. Lightweight hiking boots or sturdy walking sneakers should be worn, along with a day pack with lots of water, approximately two quarts per adult. Drink when you pause, not when you're thirsty, is a good guideline. As anywhere in Australia, wear a hat, perferrably one that will stay on in the wind. Suggested touring season is April to November, before the real heat of summer. Campers particularly should not go during the busy winter season of

June-July when heavy gear for the colder nights can be a burden.

Of Special Interest

Since this may be your only chance to experience the deep Outback, use the time to get to know the incredible history of the land and the flora and fauna as well. Guided walking tours here, given by park rangers, instruct about aboriginal food and medicine, unusual animals and how it all survives in this difficult land. Aboriginal caves and rock paintings can be found during the walk around the base of Uluru; a complete circumnavigation totals 6-1/2 miles and takes a good two hours.

Outback Adventures

A number of other off-the-wall tours are available from here. Camping on camelback and four-wheel drive treks can be arranged. Ask locally. The Northern Territory Government Tourist Bureau in Alice Springs can provide details, and can fill you in on special Aboriginal Culture Tours, run by aboriginal communities throughout the N.T.

The Outback Road

The Stuart Highway, known as **The Track**, starts in Adelaide and bisects Australia, north to south. It connects Alice Springs with its Northern Territory neighbor, **Darwin**, about a thousand miles to the north on the Pacific. Along the Track are two other main way stations, **Tennant Creek** (one-time gold mining community) and **Katherine**. Just before Tennant Creek is an interesting strange rock area. Huge rounded granite boulders are scattered across the floor of a shallow valley. Appropriately, the area has been dubbed **Devil's Marbles**.

South Australia's Outback

The dusty Outback cannot be confined to the Northern Territory. The great expanse takes up much of South Australia and Western Australia as well.

The Flinders Ranges

Some 214 miles (350 km) north of Adelaide, this razorback spine cuts the desert and shows off its marine beginnings with deposits of fossils proving this arid sandy land was once a great inland sea. Bushwalking allows tourists a good look at native animals and birds in their true wilderness habitat. Aboriginal rock paintings dot the landscape as well.

Coober Pedy

Here as in Western Australia, miners found not gold but other precious stones and reason to cut up the land. Opals support the economy here and the great holes and refuse mounds left by miners are a strange sight. Coober Pedy is almost 600 miles (960 km) away from Adelaide and only worthwhile if you are truly keen on mining and/or opals. On the way, you may catch sight of emu and kangaroo grazing, but you can do that elsewhere. Some say Coober Pedy is not so much an Outback adventure as a frontier adventure, a reminder of a rougher, earlier time.

Special note: some of the motels here are constructed underground to maintain a cool temperature in an area which can soar as high as 120 degrees.

Outback by Train

The most famous, or infamous, train in Australia is called ***The Ghan***. The overnight service links Adelaide to Alice Springs, offering a good view of the nothingness the region provides. A hot cup of tea greets you in the morning when the sun is beginning its sweltering rise. By the way, *The Ghan* was named for the Afghan camel-train drivers who plied this route in the desert. That's how the ships of the desert found themselves in Australia....people figured if they worked in the African and

Asian deserts, why not here. Now camel rides are a common family attraction.

Another train trip across the entire width of Australia is the **Indian-Pacific.** It connects Sydney to Perth, via Adelaide, and crosses South Australia's Nullarbor Plain.

Western Australia's Outback

Western Australia's economy boomed with the modern era of mining. Precious minerals of all kinds and diamonds are excavated from the earth here. Much of this arid Outback revolves around the mining communities. Western Australia covers about one-third of the Australian continent and is only populated in the fertile southwest corner near Perth (see Beaches).

Put mining aside and Western Australia's Outback offers incredible geologic formations, but remember this is a world of distances, big distances. About 155 miles north of Perth are the rock forms called **The Pinnacles** at the **Nambung National Park**. These limestone fingers which jut upward from the earth stand nine- to ten- feet tall, like stalagmites in a cave with no roof.

The Kimberleys

This is where the real excitement of strange land formations exists—but for the most part it is four-wheel drive country. Facilities in this remote region of north Western Australia are few; but intrepid campers or resourceful travelers can find accommodation if they are driven to this vast remote land. While the roads are marked, a guided tour might be the way to go.

To give you a better idea of how far away the Kimberleys are from everything: **Broome, W.A.**, on the Pacific coast is considered the eastern gateway to the Kimberley region. Broome is over 1,200 miles (750 km) north of Perth. From Darwin in the Northern Territory to the eastern edge of the Kimberleys at **Kunurra** is 560 miles (900 km) and over 1,200 miles (750 km) to the far side at Broome, W.A. The closest eastern entry point from Kunurra is **Katherine, N.T.**, 233 miles (750 km) west. If you're keen to see the region, it might be worth investing in a flight to the area.

Northern Territory

Katherine Gorge

About 240 miles (350 km) south of Darwin is Katherine, N.T. A favored destination of hikers (**bushwalkers**) and campers lies nearby. The Katherine River carved the gorge and the sandstone beds of the plateau region. Boat trips ply the river. Camping, day trips, canoe rentals and helicopter flights are listed among the choices of outdoor activities.

Like the Pinnacles, another group of bizarre rock formations draw adventure travelers. In **Bungle Bungle National Park**, great beehive-like domes of sandstone seem to have bubbled from the earth and frozen in place. Amazingly this strange territory was only charted in 1983. Its fragile landscape is being carefully protected. Bushwalkers must stick to paths following dry creek beds. The best time of the year to gain access here is from April to October.

The Green Outback

While the Centre is known as the Red, people refer to the **Top End of the Northern Territory** (and Queensland) as **The Green**. This land is tropical outback, a place where crocodiles snap, water buffalo roam and the rain forests teem with life.

Kakadu National Park

To most Aussies, exploring the rain forest region means Kakadu, one of the world's unspoiled paradises. The park entrance sits 160 miles (256 km) from Darwin on the Stuart Highway and covers over 7,700 square

feeding the animals

wallaby- yes

crocodile - no

miles! Aboriginal peoples still manage most of the park, and like Uluru, this offers a wonderful opportunity to explore the history of the earliest Australians at extensive sites, some dated to 30 thousand years ago. They depict life and native animals, some of which are now extinct. Remember only two seasons exist here: the wet and the dry, making the best travel time May through September.

Think of Kakadu as a photographic safari. In the dry season, crocs sun themselves along the **billabongs** left by the wet and can be spotted in many places throughout the park. Birdwatching tours can be arranged, and keep your eyes open for numerous reptiles, including the **goanna**, Australia's giant monitor lizard.

Difficult-to-get-to but fantastic 600- to 1,000-foot waterfalls nestle inside the park. Two-hour trips to find them pay off in stunning swimming holes and tropical Edens. Bring **togs** and a small rubber float to **Twin Falls** because you'll need to swim a creek to get there. If you can bear the trek, take a scenic flight over the region to inhale the breadth of it and the beauty.

Campers will find numerous campsites available throughout the park. No one should forget their bug spray, the little **Aussie mozzie** can be beastly.

Like the Kimberley, this might be one area to look into guided tours, sometimes called four-wheel-drive safaris. You may find it easier to be organized than to brave the huge park alone. The park service provides excellent information on the choices within the boundaries and a suggested itinerary depending on your length of stay.

Queensland

Daintree

In the tropics, north of **Cairns** in Queensland, **The Greater Daintree** and **Cape Tribulation World Heritage** national parks lure travelers into a tropical Eden. Here the rain forests touch the sea and reach out to the reef beyond the beaches. The monsoonal forests have been caught between modern enterprise and a push to save the global ecology. But it is still possible to take guided river tours which can point out plant life that date back to the age of the dinosaur. Perhaps another generation will have the same chance, if we are lucky.

Outback on the Station

The third outback category includes ranches. Huge ranches called **stations** cover much of the remaining Northern Territory, inland Queensland and New South Wales. These huge dusty places account for much of Aussie folklore, its horseman mythology, the legendary **swagman** and the Aussie **battler**. However, since stations are private land, only organized stays can be arranged. Brochures on the most up-to-date "host" farms and stations can be found at state tourist offices and information centers. Especially for families hoping to get a real glimpse of Aussie life (after all, Australia was built on the sheep's back), this may be the way to go. Some places are smaller than others. Choose what best fits your interests: dairy farm vs. sheep station vs. expansive cattle station.

Four-Wheel Drive

Many of the country's national parks from Noosa Shire in Queensland right through the tropical Top End, down through the arid Centre, in Western Australia and South Australia, the rugged hills of Tasmania and other places as well, four-wheel drive vehicles get you where you want to go. We've already noted some 4x4-only areas in this Outback section. If this rates high in your interests, check the region you are expecting to visit. Park guides can fill you in on where 4x4s can travel and on where they can be rented. Also commercial tour companies arrange four-wheel-drive safaris for individuals and small groups.

City Sights and Historic Places

In the City-by-City section, we traveled quickly around the country to taste the regional flavor of each area. Now, as you choose to narrow your focus, this section will lay out the particular sights and interests, from music to food, for which each area is noted, and locate historic points around the country.

Included in this section: Dining Out, Nightlife and Entertainment, Parks and Gardens, Spectator Sports, the Royal Shows and Exhibitions, the Arts, Museums and History.

Royal Shows, known as **The Show** in each state, equal state fairs in America. Each state capital hosts an annual show and some regional centers have smaller versions, more like county fairs.

Some historic sights, more geared to families, are included in the Family Touring chapter rather than here.

Sydney

As you fly over **Sydney Harbour** for the first time and for countless times thereafter, you will be stunned by the view of this city and suburbs that meld with the natural harbor. It seems to be an endless series of bays and quays opening onto the central waterway protected by great headlands from the pounding ocean. The harbor remains the city's lifeblood.

Climate-wise, Sydney is the most temperate of Australia's four major cities. Since weather stands out as a benefit year 'round, visitors should take advantage of any outdoor events, like festivals and concerts in **Hyde Park** or the **Domain**, as well as the obvious water-oriented activities.

The building that has taken on the onus of being Sydney's international symbol remains the **Sydney Opera House**. Its great gleaming sail-like shells dominate the downtown waterfront, offset only by the gracious **Sydney Harbour Bridge** that links the city to its northern suburbs. For Sydney in the 1970s, the Opera House proved its coming of age—this was no longer a bush capital but a cosmopolitan center. For the tourist, the inner workings of the Opera House can be inspected in minute detail. Tours offer statistics on what it cost to construct, how many bricks and tiles it took and a lengthy discussion about acoustic problems. But, the true cosmopolitan tourist would find a performance more exciting. On any evening, the bill can range from something modern to classical, from dance to New Age music.

If a big name pop band tours Australia, it plays Sydney, usually the **Sydney Entertainment Centre**.

To know Sydney, you must experience the harbour. Take a ferry across the way and back again, or better yet, hire a water taxi for lunch at a harborside restaurant, like the now famous Doyle's, for local seafood. **Circular Quay** is the main ferry terminus. The place where convicts landed two hundred years ago now services hundreds of thousands of commuters and tourists daily. In addition to short ferry rides, include a harbour tour in your itinerary. A variety of tours fit a variety of tastes but the idea is to get on the water, in the sun, for a few hours, getting to know Sydney and its history a little better.

History

The Rocks labels the original site of the first penal colony in Sydney. Today, like convicts led to their supper, tourists cannot stay away from this reborn waterfront in the shadow of the Harbour Bridge. A few historic buildings have been saved from destruction, the oldest dating to 1816, and more from the Georgian period. Streets have been spruced up and wharfside storage and factories have been turned into shopping and eating complexes. The combination creates a pleasant setting for walking tours that tell Sydney's history and provide a day of shopping, eating and imbibing. But like many similar waterside revivals in America (South Street Seaport in New York), history only takes you so far when modern commercialism takes over. Nevertheless, The Rocks cannot help being on your "must see" list in Sydney.

For more history in Sydney proper, **Macquarie Street** offers a look at colonial architecture and the first seedlings of modern free Australia.

Other historic sights outside the metropolitan area can be read about in Chapter 5.

The Pub Crawl

Nightlife can be found in any pub in town but the concentrations of nightly entertainment range from the seamier side in **Kings Cross** to the friendlier pubs and restaurants of **Paddington**. The waterfront development at **Darling Harbour** also houses nighttime events, pubs and restaurants in a semi-outdoor setting. First class hotels throughout the city also provide a setting for dining and dancing.

Art

The Art Gallery of New South Wales houses Sydney's major art collection. Included are some Australian masters—great landscape artists who captured the raw vastness of their space around the turn of the century, along with aboriginal art, modern Aussies, and international collections. A 1990s addition to the art community is the **Museum of Contemporary Art**, featuring the eclectic collection of eccentric John Wardell Power and including *avant-garde* paintings and a collection of mixed media. Smaller galleries, sought out by the serious art enthusiast, can be found scattered around the city and trendy suburbs, along with affordable art in the shops and galleries of The Rocks. Another spot to browse, the suburb of **Paddington** hosts Saturday craft fairs, offering the work of many artists who call the area home.

Museums

The Australian Museum houses the country's largest collection of natural history, including aboriginal and Pacific island artifacts. Australian history is based on its maritime foundation. Past and present come together at the **Australian National Maritime Museum** at Darling Harbour. The **Powerhouse Museum** has a large group of "hands-on" exhibits, exploring science, technology and decorative arts.

Animals and Gardens

While Chapter 5 on Family Touring includes more detail about places to see Aussie flora and fauna, it's worth noting that Sydney has a zoo with a spectacular panorama! Take a ferry across the harbour to the **Taronga Park Zoo** and enjoy the collection of Aussie and international animals in this fabulous setting. The Aquarium makes its home in Sydney's Darling Harbour area, complete with an undersea moving-walkway tunnel, becoming popular in Oz. If you do not plan to go to Queensland, where other oceanariums exist, then don't miss this one.

Like anything else on the harbour, the **Royal Botanic Gardens** commands a splendid view and is a great place to unwind at any time during your tour.

The Show

The **Sydney Royal Easter Show**, obviously held at Eastertime, considers itself Australia's largest exhibition, complete with fireworks and parade.

Sports

Sydney loves cricket and boat racing. Christmas week sees the annual **Sydney to Hobart** yacht race which fills the harbour with every imaginable craft signalling the start of the race from the harbour through the heads and down the Aussie coast. Probably the most sensational sight on the harbour all year.

Canberra, the Capital

While Canberra cannot claim to be a world city like Sydney or Melbourne, it remains a fascinating tribute to architecture and planning. The land was carved out of the Aussie bush to create a federal capital without state ties, free of rivalry. Just as for the Sydney Opera House, an international competition was held to find a person with vision, with a grand design to make this an outstanding place, with clean lines and straight forward purposes. The tale is told everywhere in Canberra that a young American architect was chosen and started the city we see today. Few people live here. Only diplomats, government employees, service business owners and employees, and **journos** (news personnel).

You can fly into Canberra in less than an hour from Sydney or travel through the bush to get there. The **Australian Capital Territory** (ACT) is nestled in a lovely section of New South Wales, en route to Victoria, but it's considered cold and windy in winter. (Of course, cold is a relative term.)

Possibly the most alluring structure in town is the newest. The **New Parliament House**, planned for the 1988 national bicentennial, sits on a rise above the old classical Parliament House and seems to slip in and out of the earth like a graceful bird on water. Once again, clean lines that blend into the landscape, rather than reaching for the stars, control the design.

Museums

Old Parliament House reopened to the public in December 1992 as a museum. Special exhibits are shown in the library, some concerning politics, others history. The lovely early 20th-century building, opened in 1927, became too small for modern government...but, oh! if the walls could talk! Some proposed it should become the National Museum of Australia, but, a committee planning that museum seems to be leaning toward a brand new structure which targets the year 2001, the centenary of the Australian federal government, as its opening date.

If your idea of seeing a country is taking in its museums, Canberra is not really the place to do it. As was said, no museum of Australian history exists. There is the **War Memorial**, which has staged life-size dioramas to depict Australia's presence in world wars and has a large collection of military paraphernalia. The **National Gallery** houses some of the finest pieces of Australian art in the country, along with a good aboriginal art collection and international pieces. This cannot be called the definitive Australian art museum, but more a way of bringing art to the Aussie people, and letting the rest of the world enjoy it as well.

The Embassies

Since this is the ultimate planned city, the international embassies have been grouped together in a kind of Disneyland scheme. Some are open to the public, displaying art and culture of their homeland; other compounds can be viewed from the roadside only. Exteriors retain the style of their country's traditional architecture. The American compound reminds you of Colonial Williamsburg in a bush setting.

The Show

The **Royal Canberra Show**, an agricultural and industrial exhibition, draws exhibiters from around the country and is held at the end of February.

Melbourne

Melbourne welcomes outsiders differently than Sydney. The aerial view is not so dramatic but once in the downtown business district, you can feel the atmosphere of this gracious city. Little **lounges** lure you inside for a cappucino and crumpet or **bickie**. **Myer**, the Macy's of Melbourne, opens onto the **Bourke Street Mall** and beckons you inside. The diversity of shopping overwhelms (and Americans will generally find clothing expensive). Local and international styles compete for window space as the trams bustle through.

Public transportation is terrific. Tram lines (like San Francisco trolleys) move people efficiently around the city (except when on strike) and connect to bus and suburban train lines. The big train stations in the city center are people size and not overwhelming. Melbourne often gets compared to Boston, another manageable place, comfortable with its history and its ethnic population.

Dining Out

While Sydney boasts of fine seafood and generally good dining, Melbourne (outside the downtown area) boasts an array of international cuisines, blended with the basics of fresh Australian seafood, plentiful veal and spring lamb. Middle Eastern cuisines rely on lamb and when the ingredients are the best the world has to offer, the recipes are lifted to new heights. Italian cuts of veal do the same, and they are not the most expensive selections on the menu because veal is not as dear as in the U.S. Oriental seafood dishes never tasted so crisp and tender as they do in better Chinese and Japanese restaurants in Melbourne. Other Asian cuisines, such as Vietnamese and Thai, have become popular here and in other Australian cities.

The only area downtown noted for food is **Chinatown** on Little Bourke Street, not far from the main mall. Try a curious walk through the district and enjoy the food selections from a number of Asian cuisines.

For other ethnic foods and fine dining generally, get

out of downtown. The Italian section of **Carlton** has restaurant after restaurant of fine food from *zuppa di pesce* to pasta and pastry. **Richmond** is known for its Greek specialties and **Brunswick** for Turkish food.

For the modern cafes (pronounced CAFF) and bistros, where b.y.o. is the way to drink, travel to the inner suburbs of **Prahran** and **South Yarra**, along Toorak Road and Chapel Street. Trams will take you there while passing some of the major sights of Melbourne. Go by day, stroll the terrific and creative shopping districts at the end of the line and stay for dinner. Don't forget to pop into a pub and pick up wine or beer to complement your meal. Some restaurants charge a corkage fee but that's little more than a tip for their trouble.

At the edge of Melbourne along the Port Phillip Bay waterfront sits **St. Kilda**. While this section has a somewhat seamy reputation after dark, it is also a place where cultures meet...and that means food as well. Discover St. Kilda on a Sunday afternoon. The **Esplanade** along the beach turns into a marvelous arts and crafts flea market; and unlike downtown, the shops along Aclund Street are open on Sundays. Here continental bakers, mostly Jewish immigrants, whose trades were learned in Europe, entice passers-by to nosh their way around the block. Chinese, Lebanese, French, Polish and other ethnic eateries fill the storefronts around the bakers. Even winter can be inviting here—rich warming foods, hot chocolates and coffees within the scent of the sea.

Nightlife

Nightlife can range from a pub with a raucous local rock band to dancing at sophisticated nightclubs or an evening in a **wine bar**. As in any city, the trendy places change regularly and must be found anew each trip. Most big name entertainers who come to Australia, do

Melbourne. Popular acts play the **Entertainment Centre**.

The Arts

Broadway-style theater, symphony and other major performances usually take place at the **Melbourne Concert Hall**, a part of the **Victorian Arts Centre**. The modern building perched on the edge of the Yarra River sports a much less dramatic facade than the Sydney Opera House, but inside, the setting is more comfortable, more amiable. The sound has always been marvelous. Perhaps that's the difference in the two cities. Sydney equals showy; Melbourne mirrors quiet perfection. Enjoy a comfortable performance; don't just tour the place. Upscale restaurants and dessert cafes can hold you in the complex for hours before or after a performance.

Along St. Kilda Road, heading south from downtown, the rest of the Centre includes the State Theater complex, Performing Arts Museum and The National Gallery of Victoria. If it's fine museums you yearn for, Melbourne is the place. This marvelous art gallery features Australian and international works in a beautiful setting (although the outside is plain). While not so overpowering as to require more than a day to absorb, its grand spaces make for fine viewing. In the same area, the **Performing Arts Museum** offers changing displays, described as imaginative and often hands on.

Museums and History

In another part of town (on the underground train loop from Flinders Street Station), the **State Library and the Museum of Victoria** were built following the Gold Rush years of the 1850s which brought prosperity to Melbourne and neighboring Victorian towns. The imposing edifice houses perhaps Australia's finest library and a museum which encompasses science and nature, a planetarium, and displays of aboriginal and Australian history. It is the kind of museum Canberra so desperately needs. Consider this a wonderful wander, if you have time.

Another smaller museum, but important to Australian culture (though many Aussies might not agree), is the **Museum of Chinese Australian History**. The Chinese settled Victoria during the gold rush as a large majority of the work force. This museum is the only place which celebrates that contribution.

The **State Houses of Parliament** represent a living museum where government can be witnessed in action. Some seasoned tourists say Victoria's Parliament offers the best tours, better than New South Wales or Canberra.

Como House in South Yarra, just a short walk from the hustle of Toorak Road, impresses the visitor as a stunning example of the exquisite residences built during the later 19th century. The house and outbuildings are all original.

Gardens and Parks

Since Victoria hails as the Garden State it would be remiss not to visit the gardens of Melbourne. Bordered by St. Kilda Road on the west and the Yarra River on the east, **Kings Domain** encompasses Alexandra Gardens (across from the State Theatre), Queen Victoria Gardens (across from the National Gallery), the Shrine of Remembrance (a war memorial) and the stunning Royal Botanic Gardens. Alexandra Avenue, a beautiful esplanade, follows the riverside edging all the gardens and creates a wide swath of picnic land and bike paths.

Near the Houses of Parliament on the hill at the top of downtown lies **Treasury** and **Fitzroy** gardens. The latter is the location of Captain Cook's cottage, shipped from England, and a miniature Tudor village. And yes, Melbourne has its Zoological Gardens too, a zoo set in a truly garden-like setting. The Melbourne Zoo rates as the third oldest zoo in the world.

Moomba and Markets

If you come to Melbourne in March, you may be treated to the Down Under version of *Mardi Gras*, a raucous two-week event on the streets of the city and along the river called **Moomba**.

Market stalls selling anything from soup to nuts, clothes and souvenirs, can be found at the **Queen Victoria Markets**. The Vic Market can be fun for those who love quasi-bargain hunting in flea markets but if time is of the essence, give it a miss, and see a museum or take a walk in the gardens instead.

If you really love to shop, Melbourne has a big outlet district on Swan Street in **Richmond**. If time allows, take a tram and go. You can plan lunch or dinner in the same area in some trendy local restaurants, an Aussie pub or in Greek or Asian places as well.

Spectator Sports

Melbourne stands out as a sports city in a country of sports fanatics. Australian Rules Football (always called **footy**), cricket, horseracing and tennis top the list of spectator sports. Footy season starts in March and the metro area goes crazy when the **Aussie Rules Grand Final**, the equivalent of an American Superbowl, winds up the season in September. On the first Tuesday of November, Melbourne and the rest of Victoria close shop and watch a horserace, the **Melbourne Cup**, at **Flemington Racecourse**. For a whole week, social events are held surrounding the Cup. The international Grand Slam tennis season begins in Melbourne at the **National Tennis Centre** in January each year. As for cricket, this most British of British games is loved by Australians, even though it takes five days to complete a match. But, the Australians, ever the forward thinking group, created a one-day cricket game, played by teams for television. They even wear colored uniforms, a big step away from traditional white.

Historic Sights Outside the City

Victoria has many fine historic towns, with architecture and quaintness dating from the 1850s gold rush days. **Ballarat** can be a long day trip or a pleasant overnight from Melbourne. Historically, this was the center of the Victorian gold rush. Today, **Sovereign Hill**, a recreated mining town, brings back life in that era better than any other place in Australia. (See Chapter 5 for more information.) Beyond Ballarat, find more goldfields territory and more lovely places to explore, including the towns of **Maldon**, **Kyneton** and **Daylesford.** All of these can be seen during an extended driving tour. Bed-and-breakfast accommodations have become popular. Book ahead through a tourist office.

Another historic section of Victoria sits on the Murray River where the state borders New South Wales. The town of **Echuca** is perhaps the most famous. Paddlesteamers ply the river near the restored wharf for tourist trips and the little main street was refurbished as the setting for a television series called *All the Rivers Run.*

Food was great when we were there. Look for lovely old-fashioned restaurants and enjoy barbecued **yabbies** fresh from the Murray. Pub accommodations, shared showers and all, made it a delightful overnight trip.

Along the southern coast, west of the Great Ocean Road, are towns which helped formulate the early years of Victoria. **Portland** was among the first settlements, started by whalers, who made their living in the rough Southern Ocean or from the whales caught there. Today, museums and early buildings bring alive the early 19th century. Nearby **Port Fairy** has a number of buildings listed by the National Trust. Similar settlements can be found along the southern coasts of South Australia and Western Australia as well.

Because of conservation, whalewatching has become a winter past time in the region. Check with locals for information about pods and viewing cruises.

Adelaide

While not counted among Australia's big three, Adelaide has a special presence all her own. People usually come here while they tour the South Australian countryside and the two prominent wine-growing regions near the city. But that's not to say Adelaide is not worth seeing on her own. Adelaide takes on the air of a storybook town—clean, well-designed, punctuated by lovely spires and adorned with hundreds of trees.

Dining

The downtown hotel and restaurant area can be walked easily and great food can be found, especially in the Italian restaurants and steak houses. Don't forget seafood—**crayfish** and **yabbies** top the list of good treats. Kangaroo is edible here, too. South Australian wine has an international reputation, so take advantage.

Nightlife

Performing arts of all kinds are alive and well in Adelaide. An old railroad station has been reborn as a casino and an old church now houses a warren of restaurants and bars with live entertainment.

Museums

Adelaide boasts a couple of good true Aussie museums worth seeing if time permits—**Old Parliament House**, a constitution museum, and **South Australia Museum**, with a large collection of aboriginal artifacts.

Gardens and Parks

As in most Aussie cities, gardens hold an important

place in the life of the town. In fact, so important here that when the original city plan was drawn the downtown business district was ringed by parkland, setting it pleasantly apart from the residential areas. The **Adelaide Botanic Garden** houses a unique giant water lily house and the country's only museum of economic botany. And Adelaide, too, has a zoo.

Sports

Adelaide hosts the **Australian Grand Prix** in October, making it a major stop on the Formula One race car circuit. No one would imagine the City of Churches being on the calendar, but so far it has proven a popular venue. Book ahead for accommodations.

May 15th is the running of the **Adelaide Cup**, a state holiday for a horserace.

Historic South Australia

Outside Adelaide, the river town of **Strathalbyn**, hosts the **National Trust Museum** in two buildings, the 1858 police station and the 1867 courthouse.

Victor Harbor, further south on the Fleurieu Peninsula, boasts a few historical museums and the **Cockle Train**, a scenic 30-minute train ride along the ocean on Australia's oldest public railway. The town was founded as a whaling site.

In the **Barossa Valley**, known for its wines, at least one National Trust Property might capture your attention as well—**Collingrove** at **Angaston**. Built and owned by the Angas family through the 1970s, the house now displays the high style of life enjoyed by **pastoralists** or landholders of the last century. Limited accommodations can be arranged to really submerge one into another era. (See the section on Vineyards for more information.)

Perth

Perth rises out of the banks of the Swan River. Gleaming modern buildings glisten in the Western Australian sun. **Kings Park** on Mount Eliza looks down from the hill on this beautiful but isolated city. While wholly Australian in the way that Fort Worth is wholly American, Perth remains distinct from other Aussie capitals. It is so far from everywhere else. In fact, Perth is closer to Indonesia than it is to Sydney. Rich iron ore deposits and natural gas in the Pilbara region continue to bring wealth and growth to the area.

The Arts and Art Museums

The city hosts the West Australian ballet and opera companies and the **Festival of Perth** (during February and March), which brings in performing artists from around the country. The **Art Gallery of Western Australia**, part of the **Perth Cultural Centre**, houses a collection of Australian, aboriginal and international works.

Nightlife

Daylife overshadows nightlife here. However, many Aussie cities are turning toward casinos to round out their tourist offering. Perth has followed suit with the **Burswood Resort and Casino**. In the downtown, clubs can generally be found in the major hotels, but most people head ten miles down river to the port of **Freemantle**. Since hosting the America's Cup yacht races in 1987, **Free-oh** cleaned up its act from a somewhat seedy port town and restored its historic sights, expanded accommodations, restaurants and pubs. Now, it's the place to be during warm Mediterranean-like evenings. It's easy to get a bus or taxi from Perth to and from Freemantle.

Gardens and Animals

Kings Park encompasses a thousand acres of lovely gardens on the side of **Mount Eliza**. Long leisurely walks and picnics with a Perth panorama highlight an afternoon above the city. Parkland along the Swan offers free access to the river below. Perth has a zoo and some family adventure parks in the outlying suburbs, including an Underwater World oceanarium.

History Alive

Western Australian Museum in Perth has a natural history collection, but more importantly, it displays the history of the state. Within the complex stands the 1856 **Old Gaol** which served as Perth's early prison and now exemplifies colonial architecture. Since Western Australia was a convict state until transportation of convicts ended in 1868, jails and prisons are common historic sights. In Freemantle, the **Roundhouse**, the original jail dating back to 1831, has been restored and boasts of being the state's oldest surviving building. In 1855, the convicts built their own sandstone prison which was in use until 1991. Today, the **Fremantle Prison** stands as a museum of itself.

Markets

Like many Australian cities, Fremantle has its markets. They are at once as old-fashioned as farmers' markets and as new as the latest trendy flea market. They furnish an opportunity for fun browsing, maybe on a rainy day, and a cheap lunch at the food stalls and shared picnic tables. Open Friday through Sunday.

Darwin

A funny little place with a small population (only 70,000), Darwin probably has a greater cultural mix than most Australian cities. Here Asians, Aborigines, Torres Strait islanders and Aussie frontiersmen coexist.

Most tourists come to Darwin because they want to explore the Top End and the rain forests. Of course, you wouldn't want to be there during the Wet, from December to April. The place is unbearable. In the Dry, during the rest of the year, the heat can be unduly harsh. Take your pick.

But whatever lures you here, there is something cosmopolitan about Darwin to be discovered. Food comes from many lands in a great selection of restaurants and the local seafood boosts any menu.

Nightlife

Nightlife comes in the form of many pubs and a casino complex.

History to Relive

On Christmas Day 1974, Cyclone Tracy virtually leveled the city and the surrounding area. Few historic buildings remain, others have been restored. So this is a very new place. For remnants of an earlier time, look for **Old Admiralty House** and **Government House**. Exhibits relating to the cyclone can be found at **Fannie Bay Gaol**, a museum of itself (and the cyclone). For one of Australia's finest looks at its aboriginal roots, see the **Museum of Arts and Sciences**.

Gardens

Darwin Botanic Gardens were first planted in the last century but have been replanted since the cyclone.

Brisbane

When we talked about beaches, we started our trek in the Sunshine State. Now we are here in the capital city of Brisbane (pronounced *Briz-bin*, not *Briss-bain*). There is an elegance to this old city, with its main plaza (King George Square) adorned with royal palms reaching for the sun. Remember, Brisbane is subtropical and the flowering trees and bushes will remind you of that at every turn. Summer can be too hot to handle if heat and humidity are not your idea of traveling companions, but spring can be beautiful (October). The dead of winter, August, can be unpleasantly wet and damp. It may not get terribly cold but since interiors, including restaurants and homes, are not generally heated and not geared for anything but staying cool, the damp can feel even colder. There is no place to get away from it.

Note: While the names of areas make you feel as though you've crossed into a suburb, you haven't. Brisbane sprawls. The city council covers probably one of the world's largest cities landwise.

The River

Like Perth on the Swan, Brisbane is situated in the curve of the Brisbane River, but like many other cities, the river was largely ignored until recent years. The **Brisbane Botanic Gardens** provide a lovely walk along the waterfront. To the south side of the river, travelers will find **South Bank Parklands**, on the former site of **World Expo Park**, the world's fair which coincided with the 1988 Bicentennial Expo celebration. South Bank's public space has been divided into several sections: a patrolled beach, swimming lagoon, concert area, a tropical rain forest, retaurants and pubs. Evening and daytime events are scheduled regularly. Various ferry and boat tours of the river can be chartered—one in a paddle steamer, another to a koala sanctuary and others that criss cross at several points.

Downtown

The main shopping district takes in the **Queen Street Mall**, a tree-lined walking mall. All shop fronts are protected by veranda-like roofs to offer a bit of shade. Outdoor restaurants and cafes (called caffs) provide pleasant chances to people watch. You'll find a cross section here. The elderly Aussie ladies (the "blue rinse set"—from the blue-gray tint of their hair dye) maintain their decorum in shirtwaist dresses and practical little sandals. Most have learned they must wear their hats all the time (because they've probably had some melanomas already removed). The gents still don knee socks, walking shorts and open-collared shirts. But they look different somehow than the white-shoe-white-belt-plaid-pants crowd you find among the American tourists. The colors are less bright or something and polo shirts noticeably missing. As for the young, trendy casual clothes fit the bill everywhere. No preppies here. Women go for no stockings, open toes and sleeveless tops. While the Queenslander prefers to wear very little, they do follow the style when it comes to skirt and shorts lengths. Blokes on their own time live in t-shirts and **singlets** (tank tops), shorts (whatever length), thongs or **sandshoes** (sneakers). Much of the gear follows surfie trends. The big retailers have tried to introduce heavier winter wear in Queensland, but it seems so incongruous with the climate that you have to wonder who buys it, except for tourists returning home to a northern zone.

The Myer Centre sparked new life into the main mall area when it opened in the late eighties. The giant mall anchored by a Myer department store was constructed behind a series of old store fronts. Inside, joyful screams can be heard coming from the roller coaster that flies around the top floor entertainment area. A great outing for the kids, if you want to shop, too.

Eateries and Nightlife

Small clubs and rowdy pubs make up the night life for most here. Downtown entertainment is spotty. Most locals go to the pubs in their areas to hear local bands. Many folks head to Surfers Paradise for hot nightlife (see Beaches section). Some interesting restaurants exist but you need to ask around, because the trendy scene is always changing.

The **Wharf at Breakfast Creek** has been home to some nice eateries (day or night) and a boat ride, but the financial fate of that complex has been in question. Ask about it, and if in doubt you can always head in that direction (east from downtown) and fall back on the well established Wharf Restaurant with its marvelous fresh seafood platters or Breakfast Creek Hotel, known for steaks served in its outdoor Spanish Gardens. More trendy dining can be found at the **Waterfront Centre** downtown with great views of the river.

Plans for a casino have been underway for many years; there's even talk of putting it in the historic Treasury building.

The Arts

Across the river from the river from downtown stands the **Queensland Cultural Centre**. The complex includes the Queensland Art Gallery, the Queensland Museum, State Library and the Performing Arts Complex. Many tours and events are held here and cafes and shops can round out your visit.

Markets

The **Waterfront Centre** hosts an upscale arts and crafts market every Sunday. **Paddy's Markets** in the **New Farm** district remind you of any flea market, only this one covers several floors of an old warehouse. Give it a miss unless you're staying in Brisbane for a long time and have a spare day, or a rainy day to kill.

Gardens and Animals

We've mentioned the Botanic Gardens along the river. More botanical gardens have been planted along **Mt. Coo-tha**, the singular hill that provides a marvelous panorama of the entire city, the meandering river and Moreton Bay. Down the side of Mt. Coo-tha are the new botanic gardens as they're known, for those who really want to explore more tropical fauna. The **Sir Thomas Brisbane Planetarium**, within the gardens, boasts of being Australia's largest planetarium. (All the major television networks have their facilities atop the mountain, where the transmitter towers reach skyward.)

One of Brisbane's biggest tourist attractions remains the **Lone Pine Koala Sanctuary**, accessible by boat ride, bus or car. While Lone Pine is a wonderful place to take a photograph with a koala and walk among a herd of tame kangaroos and wallabies, we've found it overly crowded in recent years and have been directed by Brisbane friends to **Alma Park Zoo and Tropical Park Gardens**, 17 miles (30 km) north of Brisbane at **Kallangur**, en route to the Sunshine Coast (see Beaches).

Barracking

Brisbanites love their sport (never called sports in Oz, just "sport"). **Barracking** (cheering) for the Broncos has become a way of life. The Broncos play Rugby League, a professional game. (Rugby Union is different again, played as an amateur and school sport.) Because rugby is the winter sport, the same fans quickly turn into avid cricket watchers. American basketball has caught on like wildfire in Queensland, creating local professional teams peppered with American athletes.

Historic Places

Newstead House, a forerunner to **Government House**, can be seen as part of a trip to **Breakfast Creek** (see Eateries above). The house and surrounding parkland command an outlook on both Breakfast Creek and the Brisbane River. Considered Brisbane's oldest private home, she remains the "grand old lady" of the city's historical houses. Driving along George Street, you cannot help spot a series of beautiful Victorian townhouses, now known as **the Mansions**. The building exteriors have been restored and now house a National Trust gift shop (usually good places to find quality and help support Australia's historical fund) and restaurants, but most of the space is taken by professional offices.

While **Queenslanders** is what people from Queensland call themselves, *Queenslanders* also denotes a style of house unique to this region. Look for them in your travels around the area; many have been horribly hurt by modern additions but many have been restored lovingly to their gracious beginnings. Just what is a Queenslander? you ask. They are homes built on posts, raised a story off the ground to allow air to circulate around the building, keeping it cool in the intense heat, keeping pests out. Graceful verandas wrap around the single-story structure clad in wooden weatherboard, capped by a painted tin roof. Usually, fancy lattice and gingerbread railings shade the veranda. Double doors provide the main entry but floor to ceiling french doors open from each room onto the veranda, to capture any breeze that might blow through on a sultry night. There's seldom a hallway per se, as the rooms run from one to another with large doorways. In modern times, people have enclosed "under-the-house" to create more living space but that changes the air flow. The original design remains the best and the brightest. The most beautiful Queenslanders usually are surrounded with tropical gardens dressed by lovely purple jacaranda trees and other tropical bushes adding more shade and beauty.

The Ekka

The Brisbane agricultural fair doesn't take on the name "Show," instead it's the **Ekka**! No, this is not some aboriginal word, just the truncated version of **Exhibition**. Brisbane holds a one-day holiday every August to launch the annual event.

Hobart, Tasmania

While Tassie is a little place, it offers a wide variety of historical treasures from its early days as an isolated penal settlement. There is no cosmopolitan atmosphere to lure a true city traveler and for many people on a short visit to Oz, Tasmania represents too much of a detour. But those who love Tassie, the Apple Isle, say don't consider *not* getting there.

The little city of **Hobart**, with a population of 180,000, is the second oldest city in Australia (behind Sydney) and some say it's in as beautiful a setting along a river backed by mountains. It displays one of the largest collections of Georgian architecture in Australia, offering many sandstone structures built by prisoners of the colony.

Historic Sights

Walking tours of the Battery Point district offer a wonderful look at the ways things used to be in Hobart, especially during its heydey as a whaling port.

Museums

Tasmanian Museum, built in 1863, puts Tasmania's tragedies in historical perspective. **Van Diemen Memorial Folk Museum**, named for the Dutch founder of **Van Diemen's Land** (Tassie's original name), recreates the early life here during colonial and convict days from the gentry's point of view. If you're into prisons, head for **Port Arthur**, one of Oz's most infamous spots, about 65 miles (104 km) southeast of the city. Tours of the National Park will give a better idea of the horrible conditions and extreme workloads placed upon the transportees. **Georgetown**, the port town where the Seacat (a giant ferry) boat from Victoria docks, offers a look at many historic buildings and a maritime museum.

Food

Stick to local seafood for a treat, especially the famous Tasmanian oyster, a big guy, full of flavor. They go down well with a beer chaser. Salmon and trout caught locally are just as inviting. Fresh local fruit and cheese complement any visit.

Countryside Australia

If you've been reading right through, you know by now we have covered the beaches, the outback and the cities and some historic sights which may be found in the countryside near the major cities. While there exists some overlap, this section will try to introduce you to the **Bush**. This represents the country areas surrounding the cities and bordering the Outback.

Most of this is farm country, some very green, some more harsh. But the countryside is not all sheep stations and dairy farms, pineapple plantations and cane farms. The trendy areas to explore have become the vineyards and the mountains, exposed to the world in the movie *The Man From Snowy River*. This chapter will seek to explore the variety and interests the Aussie bush has to offer.

Since Australia considers itself an agricultural nation and its heritage rides on the sheep's back, the bush (never brush) plays a big role in Australia's psyche. Much of the colloquial language (see Part II about Station Life and the Bush Telegraph) can be traced to bush roots (pardon the pun). Traditional clothing continues to be trendy city gear with the back to basics moves of this generation. So if you have the time, by car or by train, get out of the cities and see the bush.

New South Wales

New South Wales has its share of beautiful countryside from the Blue Mountains, 50 miles (80 km) west of Sydney to New England, and the Hunter Valley wine region, north of the city.

New England

There is a sign along Route 15 outside **Wallangarra** near the Queensland/New South Wales border that states: "Welcome to Glorious New England." It reminds the traveler he is in a unique region of New South Wales

AUSTRALIA

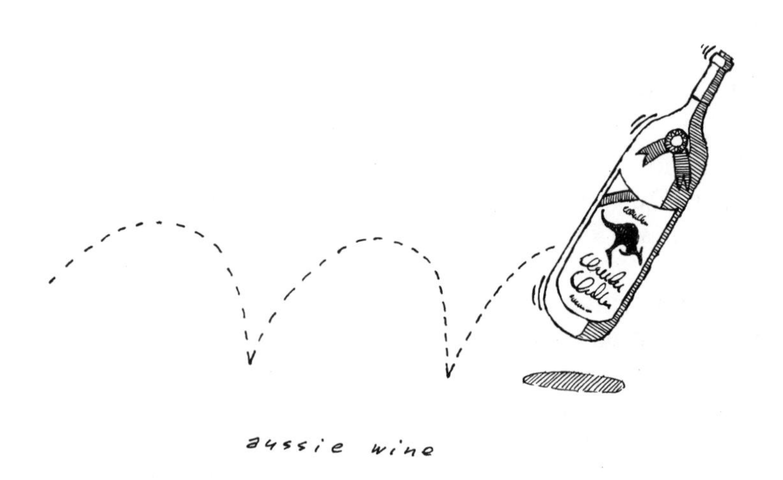

known for its rural beauty, rolling hills, country charm, four distinct seasons and a diverse history.

Tenterfield, a town made internationally known by the late singer-songwriter Peter Allen, remains the northern gateway to New England. Allen grew up there and was the grandson of the town's saddle maker about whom he reminisced in the song, "Tenterfield Saddler." The Centenary Cottage (a makeshift museum) is cluttered with history and memorabilia—pictures of the saddler and other town sons including the army solicitor who defended "Breaker" Morant (now of movie fame) in South Africa during the Boer War. A. Banjo Paterson, Australia's most famous bush balladeer and the author of the poem, "The Man From Snowy River," was married in the local church; and in the School of Arts came the first state call for federation of the Australian state back in 1889. Quite a history for one small place.

Every New Year's Day, the descendants of early Scottish settlers gather for Tenterfield's Highland Gathering, sending the skirl of bagpipes and the beating of drums echoing across the Tablelands.

Along the New England Highway south sits **Armidale** where the University of New England and the Regional Art Museum are located. The streets of Armidale compete with fine examples of Victorian and turn-of-the-century buildings frosted with lace scroll work on the verandas.

Below Armidale, attractive homesteads with traditional bull-nosed veranda roofs nestle into long rolling hills. Weeping willows line creek beds where flocks of sheep and herds of cattle seek shade.

The area's southernmost regional centre is **Tamworth**, considered Australia's country music capital. The town hosts a major festival every year.

Farm properties offer both one-day events and accommodation to those wishing to sink their hands in the dust and get their nails dirty or just to watch how work still gets done in Aussie style. Horseback riding, plenty of camping and water sports on local lakes can be found throughout the region. As always, local travel agents or tourist offices scan fill you in on the most recent information.

The Blue Mountains

The Blue Mountains are part of what is called The Great Dividing Range, the hills and mountains that separate the coast from the inland plains. **The Blue Mountains National Park** lies 50 miles (80 km) west of Sydney, making day trips possible. Bus tours head for the mountains daily from Sydney as do suburban commuter trains, but a car would give you more freedom to get out and about and possibly stay if something holds your attention for longer than you expected. Natural beauty remains a major draw to the mountains. Bushwalkers delight in the trails winding through the hills past waterfalls and forest paths.

The area remains the setting for many beautiful weekend homes built early in the century. Many of these retreats have stunning gardens (some periodically open to the public). Others have been turned into bed and breakfasts or guest houses.

Katoomba boasts of being the heart of the Blue Mountains and from there you can plan trips on the Scenic Railway that plunges into a steep valley or a skyway cable car ride, almost a thousand feet above the valley floor.

Leura has been singled out as perhaps the loveliest of the region's towns and has been classified by the National Trust. Take in the historic mansion of **Leuralla**, former home to an Australian statesman. It offers a collection of 19th-century Australian art as well as furnishings and memorabilia.

Country History

To taste Australian country flavor make a stop between the Mountains and Sydney at the **Gledswood Winery & Homestead** at **Catherine Field**, 31 miles (50 km) west of Sydney. The colonial homestead dates from the 19th Century and offers sheep shearing, sheepdog mustering and boomerang throwing exhibitions, along with horse trail rides. Check ahead. Usually it's open Sundays only. Also on weekends, in the mountains, look for the **Megalong Valley Farm**, which offers a variety of farm-life demonstrations and a petting zoo.

Wine Country

If you cannot leave Australia without sampling a bit of the grape (and many people wouldn't dare), New South Wales has its share of fine wineries in the **Hunter River Valley** region, a little over a hundred miles north of Sydney. (If you drive south from Queensland, this can be your second NSW region after New England to appreciate.)

Cessnock is the southern gateway to the valley. There you can stop at the **Hunter Valley Wine Society**. Hundreds of wines can be tested there and you can organize the rest of your trip through the valley from here. Many Hunter wineries now export to the U.S. and their names may be familiar to Aussie wine connoisseurs: Lindemans, Rothbury Estate, Tyrells, Hungerford Hill to name a few.

Most have wine-tasting tours or even longer winemaking tours. Where there is fine wine, so can be found fine food. Ask for local recommendations and enjoy your stay at a guest house or pub.

The Southern Highlands

The Southern Highlands denotes the hilly area, south of Blue Mountains National Park, 75 miles (120 km) south of Sydney and en route to Victoria. More quaint towns fill the lush green hills here. Find a tea room or two to take a break. **Bowral** is a particularly pretty little town surrounded by fancy homesteads, some of which open their gates at tulip time in October to show off their beautiful gardens.

The Snowy Mountains

Continuing south now, The Snowy Mountains start in New South Wales and cross into the state of Victoria. All these east coast mountain chains make up The Great Dividing Range. The highest peak is Mt. Kosciusko and is part of **Kosciusko National Park**. This is a rare spot in Australia. Snow falls here. People ski here and play in the snow in winter (August). The 2,600 square-mile park shows off with glacial lakes, alpine meadows and a truly unusual sight—snow gum trees. It's strange for a Northern North American to stand among leafy trees covered in snow. It's like getting snow in June when the trees are in full greenery. But it happens here and in just a few other mountain areas within the southeast of the continent.

Thredbo Village houses one of the lartest ski resorts and can be booked in advance during ski season through any travel agent. Thredbo Mountain is the only World Cup-approved Giant Slalom in Australia and therefore a draw to skiers in the Southern Hemisphere and fanatics who want to ski year 'round

When there is no snow, prices go down. Then the region offers camping, fishing, horseback riding and, of course, bushwalking.

Country Victoria

Crossing into Victoria, the mountains take on a new name: **The Victorian Alps**. This region offers Victorians their own winter playground. Well known ski areas include: Mt. Hotham, Mt. Beauty, Mt. Buller, Falls Creek and Mt. Bogong. The entire high country comes under the **Alpine National Park**. Snow buffs enjoy downhill as well as cross country skiing here.

Worldwide, however, this region took on its more

famous role in the films, *The Man From Snowy River* and its sequel. The Snowy River runs through and helps create incredible scenery, steep mountainsides where wild horses (**brumbies**) roam and sprawling stations all exist in and around the High Plains of the Alps. The history of mountain cattlemen have marked the region and today the most popular way to tour the region is in the saddle. Trail rides, day trips and even long weekend horse\camp packages are available in the High Country, some of the tours guided by the family who put together the horse crews for the movies. Since these kinds of tours and packages change, it's best to check the most recent information at the tourist board.

Falls Creek, surrounded by **Alpine National Park**, makes a good starting point for many other outdoor activities. **Mt. Buffalo** is a granite plateau, known as "the island in the sky," and home to Lake Catani.

White-water rafting, canoeing, rock climbing, abseiling, parasailing, bush walking, bicycle tours and trout fishing can all be found in the region.

Old-fashioned and modern mountain retreats offer beautiful (perhaps expensive) accommodation, but camping and motels are also available.

The Dandenongs

The **Dandenong Range** can be seen in the distance from Melbourne and has long lured Melburnians to create retreats in the lush forested land. Artist colonies grew there and one of Australia's most renown landscape painters, Arthur Streeton, built his family getaway there. Today the little towns in the Dandenongs make for wonderful day trips to explore the bush and art galleries, enjoy afternoon tea and go antiquing. On occasion, the Dandenongs get snow, changing the face of the hillsides. Among the common Dandenong destinations is **Healesville Sanctuary**, a private zoological park housing over 200 species of Australian animals.

The country setting allows visitors to roam among herds of kangaroos, wallabies and flocks of emus.

Mount Macedon and the Ranges

Another mountain escape for Melburnians, especially in summer, has been and still is **Mount Macedon**. Since bush fires destroyed so much of the hillsides in the early 80s, including homes, the region has gone through a rebirth. The town by that name has beautiful gardens and stately summer manor houses. The little streets are home to fine restaurants, art galleries and craft shops. From the summit, the Great Dividing Range is laid out before you. Turn around and find a view of the sprawling city of Melbourne and its suburbs.

If you go on a drive through the Macedon region, you'll find small wineries in this district as well, offering an alternative stopoff to the tearooms and cafes. Since the 1970s, Macedon has been known in Australia for its table wines, including Shiraz and Cabernet. While there are scenic wineries here, this is not considered Victoria's wine country. In the hills, you'll find Kyneton, mentioned in the Historic Tours section as well. Some brochures call it a "living time capsule," complete with brick and stone homes, shops and a local museum. This town saw the rebirth of local winemaking and has shepherded it ever since.

Wine Country

Victoria, historically, gave birth to Australian commercial wine growing. But its wine district in the far northwest corner of the state is certainly not as famous as the big wine region of South Australia. If you have your choice of which section to see, pick South Australia. It's not that much farther from Melbourne and offers a fine chance to see another countryside.

Rutherglen is the center of Victorian wine country, home to perhaps the most famous winery there, Brown

Brothers. But they are not alone. A handful of other winegrowers are making their name in the region as well. The Rutherglen Muscat is a prize-winning dessert wine. Many of the wineries, while offering wine tasting and tours, also offer picnic and barbecue facilities. For a vineyards romp, figure 400 (640 km) to 500 miles (800 km) round trip from Melbourne (or go to Macedon instead).

Gippsland

When discussing beaches, we mentioned the Gippsland coast, about 100 miles (160 km) southeast of Melbourne. While the beaches and the Lakes district are well known, countryside Gippsland is perhaps one of the most startlingly beautiful farming areas of Australia. Here the farms are smaller than in the big states. A big farm might be a thousand acres. Sheep live here. Cattle and dairy herds roam here. Drought, unlike in most of Australia, is rare in this part of the world, where steep hills require all of a man's skills to run a tractor, a four-wheel drive or even a horse along the tracks. But the land is green and many farms pride themselves on their beautiful gardens, filled with native and imported plants which have no trouble growing in this climate. There are four seasons but no snow. Winter is rainy and sometimes bleak, but spring and summer are gorgeous. Graziers' towns like **Korumburra** and **Arawata** have a quaint appeal and a lively day life, when every "G'day" is followed by a person's first name.

In summer, it's a shock to drive across the sunburnt flats outside of Melbourne en route to Gippsland and then find the land getting progressively green as you drive the ridges of the Gippsland Highway. Campgrounds are available as are pub and motel accommodations. Most tourists on a schedule might rather make a day trip just to see the contrast in the countryside or arrange a farm stay through the local tourist agent.

Actually, a major draw to the Gippsland region which may keep you overnight is the **Fairy Penguins** colony on **Phillip Island**. The little bluish-black penguins grow no larger than a foot tall and feed at sea all day. At dusk, like clockwork, they surf the waves into Summerland Beach and waddle up the sand dunes to burrows, where they spend the night and feed their families. It's a lovely sight, and one that is well chaperoned by parks department people who make sure the crowds do not interrupt the penguin walk. The penguins have become one of Victoria's biggest attractions. Bus tours can be arranged from Melbourne but stopping off on a trip through Gippsland is recommended. Kids will find this the highlight of the trip. But remember, evenings can be cool on the Southern Ocean, so dress accordingly.

Tasmania Is Country

Tassie remains the epitome of Country Australia. Even the small cities are rural in their feel and style. History mixes with opportunities to bushwalk and meet Australian animals and birds and take in the lovely wildflowers and cottage gardens in springtime. Orchards abound, making apples a major export of "The Apple Isle," along with apricots, small berries and wonderful cheeses. A few wineries thrive on the island.

In some ways, Tasmania has a very English country feel to it. Enjoy tearooms and small guest houses in the towns that dot the island. Historic colonial architecture and furnishings are commonplace. Bicycling tours are popular, too. (As has been said, generally short-trip travelers do not get to Tasmania; but, if you are a true lover of rural life in untouched settings, then you may want to consider Tassie seriously.)

South Australian Countryside

Most countryside tours of South Australia concentrate on the wine growing regions within an hour's drive of Adelaide, though in different directions, of course. The regions are divided into Adelaide Plains, Barossa Valley, Southern Vales, Clare Valley, Riverland, South East and Adelaide itself. Here we will touch on those of most interest for tourists on a limited schedule.

Wine Tours

South Australia's best-known country region is the **Barossa Valley**, less than an hour's drive north of Adelaide (and possibly done in a long weekend from Melbourne).

The Barossa was settled by German and Polish immigrants who worked hard and brought with them their old-world techniques of cultivating wine grapes in a climate well-suited for them. Much of the region takes on a Germanic flavor, different from other wine-growing districts. Over 35 wineries dot the valley—some large and heavy in tradition, others more modern and small. A warmth of community and spirit dominate. This is Australia at its best— people working hard to create a pleasant product of which they are proud and creating a sideline tourist industry as well.

The Barossa is known for fine food, both modern cuisine and German-style. From sausages to Black Forest cake, the menus whet any appetite.

Driving around the valley, you can see the German architectural influence. Low stone barns, unlike the sheds of most of Australia, show their age. Cottages with low doorways, small windows and steep roofs reminiscent of the harsher climate back in Germany, belie the South Australian sun. **Bethany** was the first German settlement established in 1842 and is today a quiet little burg boasting only pretty shops and an historic past.

The Seppelt family arrived in the 1840s and has become one of Australia's largest wine producing companies, complete with a well-known line of fortified wines (ports and sherries) as well as table wine. At **Seppeltsfield**, the **Seppelt Winery** is quite an attraction, from its date palm-lined drive to wine tasting tours and horse-drawn carriage collection.

The Seppelts are far from alone here. Other internationally known wines made in the Barossa include: Hardy's, Penfold's, Wolf Blass and Kaiser Stuhl.

Meanwhile, **Angaston** embodies an English heritage. One of the founders of South Australia, the Angas family, settled in the Barossa and built **Collingrove**. In its heyday the homestead oversaw 14 million acres of pastoral land (a size almost impossible to imagine). Today, it is a National Trust site, open to the public as a historic house and offering limited bed-and-breakfast accommodations in the former maid's quarters. If you are traveling without children and are lucky enough to find a free room at Collingrove, take it. Certainly, it can be the hightlight of your tour, as long as you don't mind sharing a bathroom with another room and can spend the night without television. Wine on the veranda at sunset will make up for all the inconveniences.

Artists and craftsmen settled here as well. In between wine tasting stops, browse for local pottery and other handmade items. You might find a special treasure.

An hour south of Adelaide on the Fleurieu Peninsula sit the **Southern Vales**. The center is **McLaren Vale**. Over 30 labels make their homes in this area, more Australian in character than German, but lacking in that ethnic theme that makes the Barossa so interesting. Again, travel between the wineries, tasting as you go. Plan a fancy dinner with a great wine complement or pack a picnic basket and relax outdoors in the shade of a gum tree.

The Murraylands

The **Murray River**, Australia's longest river, which flows from New South Wales and Victoria into South

Australia, was the historic lifeblood of this region. Not only did it provide much needed water for agriculture, the river was the main thoroughfare for trading and travel. Now the role has shifted. The Murray now provides leisure activities for the communities which were once layover towns for paddle-steamers and barges carrying wool and other goods from the stations to the towns and back again. Almost every town has houseboats for hire, as well as fishing trips and paddle-steamer tours on the river. Day trips or extended paddlewheel cruises leave from the towns of **Renmark**, **Mannum** and **Murray Bridge** at the Victorian border.

In many areas gum forests line the banks and fish and fowl remain abundant.

As mentioned in the historic section, Victoria's reconstructed **Echuca** shows these Murray towns for what they were in the last century and offers many of the same tour options as its South Australian counterparts.

Western Australia

Countryside Western Australia is basically confined to that southwest corner, where we found the beaches so pleasant. It's here that the wildflowers dramatically color the landscape in spring and where the rich soil and Mediterranean climate nourish grapes on the vine.

Margaret River

Margaret River is a town and a region, about a four-hour drive from Perth. Most wineries open for wine tasting and a chance to purchase wine for a night's meal. In the heart of the town, the **Old Settlement Craft Village** offers blacksmith demonstrations and handcrafts for sale. The buildings are based on Australia's group settlement farms from early in this century. (This town is situated only about ten miles from the ocean.)

En route, many people make stops in the great forests

of the west. Counted among the world's tallest trees, the **karri** are unique to this part of the world.

If you are a spelunker at heart, a wealth of impressive limestone caves can be explored. Caves Road rides the coastline and turns in toward Margaret River. Well-known caves include **Yallinggup**, **Lake** and **Mammouth** caves.

Avon Valley

About an hour's drive west of Perth sits the agricultural Avon Valley. This area is listed among the lovely wildflower displays seen from September to November. Noted towns to include in a journey through the region are **York**, **Northam** and **Toodyay**. York boasts a downtown with turn-of-the-century buildings and a **Motor Museum**, housing many models of vintage cars and carriages. Woodworking and **leadlight** (stained glass) making are demonstrated in local shops by full-time craftsmen.

If you haven't had a chance to experience Aussie farm life yet, the **Balladong Farm Museum** offers a chance to see hand shearing of sheep and blacksmiths at work.

Also, for a different experience, you can try hot-air ballooning or camel trekking. Just ask.

Queensland's Hinterland

Behind the **Sunshine Coast** lies the **Hinterland**, an area known for its stunning ridges and miles of sugar cane fields divided by twisting rivers. While the sweeping ocean beaches are not far away, this area offers its own enjoyment and leisure opportunities.

Highway One, known as the Bruce Highway, takes you from Brisbane north through this family region. Just above Brisbane, the first unique sights you will see, out to the left, are the strange peaks of the **Glasshouse Mountains**, said to be named by the early explorers. In this case, "glasshouse" stands for the mud/clay kilns used to fire glass. There is a scenic roadway through the mountains, but it takes longer to get north that way.

The Big Pineapple announces the beginning of the **Sunshine Region**. This mega-fruit stands on the grounds of a tourist attraction (and I say that meaning "trap") that introduces visitors to local fruit and nut growing enterprises. **The Sunshine Plantation** is a family place and worth a short stop if you need a break at this time. Other similar places in the region include **Super Bee**, a small fun park and bird sanctuary which tells the tale of honey making, their primary function. Many of these roadside attractions service visitors during school holidays who plan a long stay and are looking for family diversions.

Near **Nambour**, the regional center, sits the **Moreton Central Sugar Mill** which explains how cane is turned into sugar. You may catch a glimpse of the **cane tram** or its tiny tracks. Like little mining cars, the tram would pick up at local farms and take the cut cane to the mill.

Straight north on the highway, you will come upon **Eumundi**, a good pub town to unwind in. For part of this drive you will find yourself atop the **Blackall Ranges** from where you can see the Maroochy River wind through the region, once home to barges connecting farms to the towns on the coast. From up there, especially nearing sunset, you will see thick black smoke coming from the fields. The cane is burning. There is no need for alarm. Farmers burn cane before they cut it. It gets rid of the extra growth from the stalks as well as the dangerous **nasties** which slither around the bases of the plants.

Inland from **Noosa** (see Beaches), the Noosa River connects a series of lakes. **Cooloola National Park** fills a large part of the region. Escorted safaris can be arranged as can water cruises throughout the lake system or the **Everglades**.

What's to eat? As in other areas, look for fresh fruit

and vegetables and seafood in season. Crabs are **beaut** and **avos** fall from the trees. Enjoy.

Behind Surfers

The Gold Coast Hinterland offers a number of rain forest walks and scenic mountain tours. **Lamington National Park** has stunning waterfalls and **National Arch**, and at **Mount Tamborine**, with the help of rangers, visitors can find 15-thousand-year-old palms, perhaps the oldest living species the world has known.

Farms Stays

Queensland is a huge state. So when you get **back of beyond**, distances are too great to do by car unless your time is absolutely unlimited or you have one particular destination. Many stations and farms have been set up for guests throughtout the region, but because their accommodations vary so greatly, precise information about short-and long-stay properties will be left to local tourist boards. Many brochures are available and they can help you locate the kind of place and location just right for you and your traveling companions. By all means, if you have the opportunity to stay on an Aussie farm, do it. You will feel you have really tasted life Down Under.

Chapter 4

Families Going Down Under

This could be the longest trip of your life, halfway around the world with your family in tow, an exciting vacation with so many things to plan. It's best to be prepared for all travel options from the start.

Families are welcome everywhere in Australia. Remember this is a casual country. Parks, picnic areas, playgrounds, clean toilet "blocks," public beaches with water taps and outdoor showers contribute to an easy stay. Theme parks and small tourist attractions lay near every major city or resort community. Sanctuaries, zoos and nature parks draw young and old to experience the uniqueness of Australia's feathers, fur and fins.

Planning: Selecting an Airline and Getting There

There are pros and cons to almost all the five major carriers to Australia. You can read about some of them in the Planning section (Chapter 2). This section will prepare you specifically for getting Down Under with an **ankle biter** or **bub** in tow.

Most airlines pre-board families, letting you get a little extra cargo space and a chance to get settled before

everyone else. Listen for the gate call, so you do not miss it. Most will allow an umbrella stroller to roll right to your seat. Take advantage. Never attempt to travel without one if you have a young child, even a tiny infant. One exception to the stroller rule is the domestic airlines in Australia. Their carry-on rules are very stringent—one small bag per person, including children. Strollers must be checked through. (A real problem if you find yourself racing from international flight to a domestic connection Down Under and someone is trying to take the stroller from you at the last second!)

If you must fly to Los Angeles on a domestic airline and connect to an international carrier, you must remember you will have to change terminals. It is a walk outdoors from one to the other. You may want to carry a blanket to wrap around an infant or make sure you have shoes and a light jacket for older children (especially if they are traveling in pajamas). It's worth having that stroller on board to make the transfer if you have a sleepy child (four or under) with you.

Children's Fares

There are two catagories: Infant fares for babies and toddlers under two years and children's fares for ages two to eleven. In most cases infants can fly for 10 per cent of adult fares and kids qualify for a 33-percent discount or 67 per cent of the adult fare, subject to variations depending on discounts and time of year. Check individual carriers.

Note about travel with infants: You are allowed to fly with a so-called lap-sitting infant for the 10-percent fare. This child has NO reserved seat. You cannot request special food because the child is considered non-ticketed; in fact, if food is limited inflight, he may not be given a meal at all. It's up to the crew's discretion. If the plane is crowded, your child must sit on your lap for the entire flight. If there are empty seats on the plane, you may be given an extra seat as a courtesy, but that does not guarantee your family will be able to sit together.

In case of an emergency, especially with a toddler, the lap-sitting position is unsafe. A child shoud never be buckled under an adult's belt on a person's lap. Both can harm the child. Consider these things before you consider the cost of travel. (Personally, I would never fly (again) without fully-ticketed seats for all children and a car seat.)

More about Car Seats and Family Seating Arrangements

Many airlines now allow families to bring car seats on board. However requirements vary. But all airlines agree: If you do not pay full child's fare, you cannot reserve space for a car seat and an airline will not guarantee you will get to use it on a discounted seat.

In general, make sure your car seat is FAA aproved. Most name brands are these days; just make sure you don't have an old car seat made before the 1980s. More recent models have approval stickers on them which explain their use. Find the label and mark it with tape so you know where it is in case someone asks. Again for safety, I recommend bringing a seat for a child two or younger. Most children get used to their car seats in a vehicle and know it means they will be sitting for a long time. It's easy to tie, clip or Velcro toys and a bottle strap to the seat belt. This keeps things in reach and from rolling down the aisles of an airplane. Your child sits higher to look around so he doesn't feel he is stuck down in a great big cavern. If the child falls asleep, the parents know the child is secure enough so they can stretch or sleep themselves.

A couple drawbacks exist. The tray table will not open in front of a car seat, so eating can be a little more difficult. Again, as for adults, if your child is no longer using a baby bottle, bring a sports "sipper" to stop spills; and attach it to the car seat straps so you always know where it is.

Just a note about requesting seating for a car seat: Check with each carrier before you fly—domestic connections, too. If you do not need a bassinet as well, then heed these seating suggestions. Do not sit in the bulkhead. The armrests do not go up and therefore children cannot cuddle on someone's lap. Also, the bulkhead puts you under the movie screen and you may be concerned that your little bobbing head is annoying the rest of the passengers. It probably is.

If your party includes four people, ask for two pairs of seats, behind each other. It makes for easy access to the aisle for both adults or older siblings. The car seat will go against the window and not block any access. It allows for games of hide-and-seek over the back of the chair within the family and not with some stranger disinterested in your beautiful children. If your family consists of "and-baby-makes-three-or-five-or-six," choose the seats near a window and the adjacent aisle seat/seats. Both adults can get up and down easily and can access the overhead compartment. Mother and Dad can take turns being in the out-of-reach-seat for a moment's R & R. (If the window rows equal three seats, try to finagle a courtesy seat across the aisle.)

On one long flight we were given four seats across the middle for the four of us-two adults and two three-and-under. While terrific, the car seat made access to our other small child difficult and we found ourselves at times circling the plane to get to the other side, so as not to disturb a sleeping child. Some domestic airlines will not allow a car seat in the middle because it restricts egress.

General seating rule: get pairs of window/aisle seats, one behind the other and/or the adjacent center aisle seating.

Airline Family Services

Here we described potential family services provided by the five airlines. Then we will outline what each airline offers.

Children's Meals: Most airlines now offer special kids' meals, but they must be requested in advance. The best time to ask is when booking the seats and then check again about 24 hours before your flight. Check for each leg of your journey. The meals are usually limited to fried junk food or the optional peanut-butter-and-jelly sandwich, but most airlines try to accompany this with a piece of fruit or yogurt, dessert or snack, and a juice or milk container. You can ask about optional toddler and baby meals; somtimes they are available.

Infant Needs/Bassinets: Two kinds of bassinets exist: bulkhead and carrier-style. Parents with infants less than seven months or up to 20 lbs. can request seating with a bassinet.

The bulkhead type pulls out like a drawer from the bulkhead wall, usually under the movie screen. These are available at the 10-perent fare but only on a few airlines. They allow "Mum" a little freedom and the knowledge that the baby will not roll off the seat while sleeping or lying on its back. They are compact and not very deep, so a child who rolls around a lot or lifts himself up may be too cramped. I suggest you try it for size. The child cannot be in these for takeoff or landing.

The carrier-style is narrow enough to rest on the floor near parents' feet or across a couple of spare seats when possible. While it doesn't offer "extra" space to the family, it is worth using.

Infant Needs/Changing Tables: Some planes have fold-down shelves in the lavatories which transform them into a baby-changing station. That's a nice alternative to changing a diaper in a crowded aisle. Your seat neighbors will be happier with your child, too.

Infant Needs/Refrigeration: Parents carrying bottles, open baby food jars or special medicine may want to ask for refrigeration space on board, but since this is not usually guaranteed in advance, it may be better to carry a small insulated bag and cold packs. Sometimes, a caring crew member who cannot technically offer refrigeration, will refreeze a cold pack, so bring a spare to rotate.

Diaper Bag to Go: The international carriers come equipped with spare **nappies** or **nappy packs**. If you don't know, these are diapers, in this case, disposable diapers. The "packs" include disposable bibs, cleansing wipes, cotton balls and swabs, lotion and other care products which you may have forgotten or put in a cranny at the bottom of the carry-on bag and only available by emptying the entire contents.

Kids' Gift Packs: Most airlines offer children coloring and activity books, drawing materials, little "wings" or other diversions. Even if you brought your own and haven't seen any offered to your child, ask about them for the children's sake. Having a crew person give them a "new present" and recognize their presence can give a special thrill. Midway through the flight is a good time to ask, if you haven't received any attention before then. Sometimes unknowing crew may think a toddler too young for coloring and won't offer. That's up to the parent to decide. Playing cards may be available. If you ask nicely and if time permits, a pleasant crew member may offer a tour of the aircraft, but there are no promises.

Qantas

Qantas offers very good family services. If one empty seat exists in a family row, they try to hold the entire row to give the group a little extra space. If that cannot be done in advance, then a crew member will try to arrange it on board.

Fares: Under twos can fly for 10 per cent. They offer a second seat belt, which connects to the front of the adult belt, for the infant's protection during takeoff and landing especially. (However, that is still not the safest position for a child to be in.) Ages two to 11 fly for 67 per cent of the adult fare (subject to variations with discounted fares).

Car Seats: Book car seat space at time of reservations. Car seats can only be used in a reserved seat. Your reservations clerk may ask for the make and serial number of the car seat. It's best to have the information available.

Children's meals: Meals can be pre-booked at least 24 hours in advance but no peanut butter here. That's just not Australian! Infant and toddler meals offered. Your pre-schooler might prefer the toddler meal, since it is easier finger food than what is offered to the older kids. Good-sized portions.

Infant needs: Each lavatory has a baby changing shelf. At least four bulkhead bassinets exist on jumbos and are offered first come, first reserved. Refrigeration space can be made available and often jars of baby food and juices are offered. Nappy packs are always available and frequently offered, though the diapers only come in medium and are not up to the latest American standard. (But in a pinch...)

Gift packs: A series of age-related activity books, complete with punch out travel games, Aussie-theme coloring books and even hand puppets appear at intervals during the flight.

Air New Zealand

Fares: The 10-percent and 67-percent fares hold.

Car seats: FAA approved car seats can be used in reserved seats only.

Meals: Children's meals must be ordered at least 72 hours in advance of flight.

Infant needs: Nappies can be found on board along with some other baby products.

Gift packs: Kids' activity packs are on board. At time of writing, there was talk of an inflight children's headphone program but no scheduled beginning. You may want to ask about it. American Airlines airs it during Pacific flights (to Japan) and travelers say it's a great diversion.

Continental

Fares: Children 2 to 11 pay 67 per cent of the adult fare (subject to variations) and babies under 2 can fly for 10 per cent.

Car seats: Continental requires FAA approval and allows only one car seat per row. Car seats can be used only in a ticketed seat and it's best to tell the reservations clerk at the time of booking.

Meals: Kids' junk food or baby food meals available. Order 12 hours in advance of flying. Specify child's age.

Infants Needs: Bulkhead bassinets are availabe but requests are handled at the airport and cannot be guaranteed. There are no changing areas, no refrigeration space available and no emergency diaper bags. (They will supply diapers if you request them in advance. I suppose that's if you are planning to forget them!)

Gift Packs: Coloring activites offered.

Northwest

Fares: Children's discounts are not pre-set across the board like Northwest's competitors. Instead you have to check if discounts are available at time of ticketing. Lap-sitting infants may be allowed to fly free.

Car seats: FAA approved car seats can only be used for reserved seats. An approval label must be clearly attached to the seat.

Meals: Kids' food needs to be pre-booked at least 24 hours in advance.

Infant needs: No bassinets, no diapers and no changing tables exist inflight, but refrigeration space may be provided at the flight attendant's discretion.

Gift packs: Enough available to give children an added diversion.

United

Fares: Same as most competitors: 67 per cent and 10 per cent.

Car seats: FAA approved car seats can be brought on board both for reserved and non-reserved seats. A family will be allowed to use a seat for a non-ticketed infant if there is room on the plane. Otherwise, the seat will be stowed in an overhead compartment.

Meals: Children's and other special meals can be booked up to six hours before flight time.

Infant needs: Carrier-style bassinets are available on board the aircraft. There are no changing areas and no refrigeration space offered, not even for medication. Don't forget your own diapers.

Gift Packs: Junior wings and fun packs with pencils and activity books are given readily to young flyers.

Family Packing

Carry ons

For Everyone: Bring refillable sports bottles for drinks, individual cassette player and headphones, age-appropriate story, book and music tapes and creative books and reading materials. Remember toiletries: non-aspirin pain relievers, disposable moistened towelettes, tissues, lip and skin moisturizers (kids-oriented ones) and toothbrushes and paste. Bring an extra set of clothes and underwear; and a pillowcase or substitute for each person. Consider carrying a small insulated bag containing a half-dozen frozen juice boxes and holders along with small snacks varying from healthy to just fun! It's easy to get hungry between meals or between flights.

Don't forget a small flashlight per troupe. It may prove invaluable for finding some toy or book that has slipped into the dark void below your feet.

Parents with small children should add somthing extra in their own carry-on bag—a second spare shirt. You never know when a child will spill something, or spit up. Clean clothes make the entire flight more pleasant. For this reason, ladies may want to forego jumpsuits in flight. Jumpsuits are difficult to change in a crowded space and take up more room in your bag if you must change into something else.

Infants & Toddlers: Two small bags generally work better than one. In fact, three may be the answer. (Stay with me.) Remember, to reach things in flight you will find yourself rummaging around upside down under a seat for the most part. It's best to have something small enough to pick up and put on your lap easily.

A standard diaper bag should be equipped with about 10 diapers (and maybe two spares stowed in Mom's bag) and four to five changes of clothes. I recommend two-piece sweatsuits. Add several bibs, travel-size rash cream, moisturizing lotion and powder, a zipper-style plastic bag full of wet wipes, five empty large disposable zipper bags to hold a damp washcloth and potentially wet clothes and bibs, two soft receiving blankets double as sheets on the rough seat surfaces and paper pillow-cases, and/or a couple of cloth diapers for the same reason. Add tissues, infant pain reliever, decongestant and several pacifiers if needed. (Pack a new spare or two in your suitcase as well. American brands can be very expensive and hard to find overseas.)

For convenience in flight, put a few wipes, your cream, powder and any other changing essentials in a little bag on top or in a waist pack so you won't be searching for it all the time, especially for nighttime changes.

Babies need a lot of liquid in an aircraft. It's suggested they nurse or drink during takeoff and landing whether it's feeding time or not. This keeps their ears from hurting. The extra liquids mean extra diapers and extra changes. At four months, my son almost drowned. Everytime I checked his knit pants and T-shirt were wet! He was in disposable diapers but I couldn't imagine having to change him so often until it was too late. My normal routine was out of whack and because I hadn't gone anywhere or done anything, I forgot to check the diaper after each bottle or nurse (and on a crowded plane with no changing areas, you try to do it as infrequently as possible!).

I suggest two-piece interchangeable suits because you can change a bottom when the bottom is wet and, chances are, between spills and spitups, the tops will need changing, too. Knits double as pajamas unless your child will sleep better following some version of a bedtime regimen. It did not matter to my children.

Also, plan an insulated bag for your bottles or sports sippers. If your baby is still on formula, prepare four formula bottles and take something to keep them cold, and at least two water bottles. You can buy spring water in small plastic bottles in case you run out, or some prepared baby juice bottles on which you can screw nipples. (Some airline bars offer spring water, too, but you may not like the juice selections.) Carry a bottle tender—a collar which fits around the bottle neck attached to a strap with a snap on it. You may be using one for your stroller already; if not, get one for the trip.

Nursing mothers should plan bottles of formula/breastmilk and water. Sometimes, I found my seat arrangements comfortable for nursing and other times I did not. I was not comfortable in all terminal areas either. Also, you may not be ready to feed on takeoff, or if there's a delay, you may have just fed the baby and must resort to water to help prevent ear problems. When my son was four months and I knew I was heading overseas for a month, I chose not to wean him. I kept him off solid foods and nursed the whole time. It was great. In the Australian heat, I did not have to worry about formula spoiling or the water to mix formula in different areas, or unfamiliar formula brands. Also, Aussie Mums have always breastfed. No one expects anything else. One other suggestion for nursing mothers: extra shirts and nursing pads! Your nursing schedule may get thrown off by the traveling and you may find it necessary to change more frequently than usual.

The final mini-bag should be for toys, so you do not find yourself rummaging through the diapers. A backpack might help your mobility. (See toy suggestion.)

Little Kids: Even if little travelers tossed away diapers eons ago, you may want to consider asking them to wear disposable undies (if they still fit) or heavier training pants and packing spares in the carry-on. Airline toilets can be horrible places—noisy, smelly and cramped. They give some kids the heebie-jeebies. So for comfort and protection, plan for the worst. Still consider carrying a familiar blanket along with a pillow cover. A change of sweats and a clean outfit for arrival will make your child more comfortable. If a bedtime routine will make sleeping easier, bring favorite pajamas. Have your child bring a familiar stuffed toy or doll (even if that's not always a part of the bedtime routine). A "sleep-friend" to snuggle with may become important on a noisy dark plane.

Seven-plus: This age group starts to fit the "everyone" category and can manage with fresh clothing and basic toiletries. Younger children may still like to have a sleep-friend in tow.

Inflight Toys and Activities

A day or two before you go, hold a household search. Overturn toy boxes and storage bins, and have the children (if old enough) help pick out things they have not seen for awhile and may find renewed interest in. Immediately pack them into their individual backpacks to take the trip as quasi-new toys. Check travel games for pieces. If something is missing, make new bits or "borrow" from a non-travel toy for an assortment (as long as you won't worry about losing them and are willing to reciprocate).

For pens, pencils, scissors, etc., carry soft zippered pencil cases. They won't breakdown like cardboard or plastic and should make it through the entire journey. Old-fashioned fabric ones may be your best bet. They can be decorated inflight with "surprise" stickers or fabric markers.

Backpacks are a good choice for kids' carry-on bags. They can either use their schoolbags or get new ones for the trip. Encourage them to decorate the packs as you go with metal badges, souvenir buttons or sew-on/iron-on patches. (The choices will depend on your budget.) All children can carry their own and bags should never weigh more than the child can hold comfortably.

BIG TIP for older babies and children of all ages:

Bring brightly wrapped "colorful surprises" along. Nothing elaborate. Just find small books or toys, action figures, new Barbie accessories, age-appropriate puzzles, audio tapes, cards and travel games. Wrap them in layers of colored tissue and offer them as special presents when the "are-we-there-yets" begin. With older children you can make it a game of "pass the parcel," with clues under each layer about what the final surprise will be. For the little ones, the excitement of unwrapping will fill lots of time.

Infants & Toddlers: Bring brightly colored shape and rattle toys that can be tied to the car seat. Mini-busy boxes and stroller toys which can attach to the seat create good distractions (not too noisy). As soon as the child is old enough to doodle, consider one of those magic-slate-type toys—a number of brands are on the market in travel sizes. They use magnetic pens to write instead of lead and paper. Make sure pen is attached to game. Colorful cards can be fun to play matching games.

For more involved game ideas try the book **Traveling Games for Babies** by Julie Hagstrom (A & W Visual Library/New york/1981). New copies may not be available, so look in the children's department of your library. It illustrates game ideas for little ones six months to five years.

Little Kids: The four-to-seven-year-olds can be a fun age. They have more imagination and greater attention span. They can turn play into art. Keep this in mind. Bring magic things with you like a couple of colorful bandannas or scarves (for you and them) to become costumes or hand puppet outfits. Make sure you have washable markers, plastic safety scissors, glue sticks, stickers, colored paper or cards. Card stock in bright neon or other colors can be turned into wonderful postcards to send to friends. Bring a stenopad or some other notebook to begin a scrapbook/diary of your trip from the very start. Children can begin by cutting maps and other airline details out of the inflight magazines or asking for crew autographs. Older children can write notes about the day or descriptions of the pictures they've found. Paper lunch bags can be turned into easy puppets, too.

Reusable vinyl stickers (like Colorforms®) can be found in many variations. A company called UniSet® offers them in flat easy-to-carry folders. Themes include an airport (how appropriate!), circus, dinosaurs and many others. Other companies offer similar "paper" dolls or world maps.

Bigger Kids: Scrapbooks work well with this crowd, too. Make sure they've selected their medium before leaving. This age may be more interested in headsets and tapes they've chosen and maybe a surprise new tape gift when the trip seems too long. Brain teasers and hand-held electronic games and involved activity books are good for play, depending on the kids. Good books can be a godsend. Visit the library with older children before you go. Notice the kinds of books they find interesting. Then narrow down to new titles and subjects. Maybe allow each to buy a new book or two before leaving. A friend suggests scanning children's magazines to which you may already subscribe and tear out sections that have not been read or "done." These take little space and can be discarded when used. Save the most recent issue just for the trip. Some family magazines have kids' sections, too, which children don't usually see. Clip those.

Barbie® dolls may be your best bet if that's what keeps your daughter occupied. If so, one mother suggests leaving tiny shoes home. One good excuse—everyone likes to go barefoot in Australia! It might work. Once again, a zippered case or a slightly larger cosmetic bag may be enough to pack a doll or two and a few accessories so they can be extracted without trouble from the mixed media in the backpack.

Reminders: It is not only a long trip going but a long trip returning home as well. Some of the same tips apply. If your children have collected a few new things along the way to play with inflight, pack already-read books or over-used games in your suitcase. Some "tired" toys you may choose to leave behind. But the colorful surprises tip still stands. Perhaps you can keep an eye out for a few new things as you travel to wrap for the return.

Also, remember to collect scrapbook materials. The return flight is a great time to catch up on diaries and scrapbooks while events remain fresh in everyone's memory. You can exchange ideas and fill in the blanks. (It is a good idea to keep a simple calendar of "when and where" while you're moving around.)

Suitcases

I cannot say that I am the best packer. I have learned by trial and error. Packing for a family is easier in some ways. It makes you more practical. Do not try to impress anybody with your child's wardrobe on a trip of this kind. Remember it's casual and chances are it will be hot or at least warm.

Keep in mind, children's clothes are generally more expensive in Oz than in the U.S. and the selection not as great. Bring what you need and plan only to fill in with souvenir t-shirts, hats and in some cases shorts. May is a good month for sales at the beach resorts. Swimsuits and beachwear will be at season-end prices. But otherwise, few deals exist.

One exception is cotton pajamas. Since the flame-retardancy consumer rules do not exist in Australia, cotton flannel and cotton knit and cotton/poly blend pajamas can be purchased at reasonable prices. Also, the Bond's brand offers terrific infant jumpsuits made primarily of looped cotton terry. A little nylon is added for strength (like in socks). Other Bond's cotton baby underwear, especially ribbed singlets and terry-footed pants and tights, wash and wear extremely well.

Sunburn prevention: Basically, we've covered toiletries for everyone, but it should be stressed: DO NOT FORGET THE SUNBLOCK FOR THE WHOLE FAMILY. In addition, prepare your children to wear hats all the time. Let them bring fun headgear along and let them know they will not go out in the sun without it. Australian schools will not let children take recess without hats. School hats are not only traditional, but now have become mandatory for skin-cancer prevention. If you can, allow the kids to buy a new hat or cap during the trip so they have a choice about what to wear.

Infants: Think cotton. While Aussie babies seem to live in singlets (sleeveless undershirts) and fluffy diaper covers, that's not enough protection for a traveler's skin. Seersucker and similar weight long pants/overalls, lightweight cotton jersey snap-front shirts, snap-leg rompers or pull-on pants offer more protection and comfort. They will keep the baby from sticking to hot seats. Sunsuits make cute changes, but the sun may be too strong. There's nothing worse than a baby with sunburn.

Everyday: Two pairs of lightweight slacks or jeans, three pairs of shorts, five t-shirts, two long-sleeved shirts, six pairs of undies and socks should be enough for anyone. Women and girls may want to add a sundress or substiture a denim skirt for a pair of shorts. Men and boys may want a nice polo shirt for that mandatory dress-up day. A cotton cardigan goes a long way when the kids need to looked "scrubbed." Add two swimsuits each.

Footwear: Everyone should have comfortable walking sneakers. Break them in before the trip, so blisters do not spoil any fun. Good light-colored cotton socks will let feet breathe but may have to be changed in the course of a hot day. Pack at least six to eight pairs per person.

Each person should have a pair of sandals for a change and at the very least a pair of open beach thongs or jellies.

If you plan to be on the reef, bring old sneakers or aqua-shoes for foot protection. (One suggestion is to bring really rotton canvas sneakers with you, so you can throw them away at the end of your reef tour. But they need to be strong enough to keep the nasties from stinging or scratching your feet.)

Bring hiking boots only if you plan serious hiking, though a high-top sneaker or lightweight boot may be good for extensive bushwalking. If you plan a farm stay, the kids might need **gumbies**—rubber boots. Pick them up in a farm town at a second-hand shop and leave them behind when your stay ends. The place you are staying may even have a collection to borrow from.

Sleepwear: For kids, you've included a sweatsuit for the plane ride, which can double as warm gear for evenings or pajamas. But you may also want to pack cotton long johns for sleeping. Evenings can get cool (sometimes) and that gives you a comfortable pajama option as well as a spare long-sleeved t-shirt.

Pack what you find comfortable.

Outerwear: A zip-up sweatshirt jacket or hooded pullover may be the heaviest weight you'll need. For travel during winter, you may want something a little more substantial—a waterproof jacket with a poly lining, like a Lands' End Squall or its equivalent from L.L. Bean or Eddie Bauer. They served us well in August in the mountains and countryside of Victoria. Usually the sweatshirt hood will serve as a hat but you might want a poly-fleece style cap or a light-weight winter hat.

OZ ZOO
emu
wombat
quokka
kanga
koala
grub
bandicoot

Chapter 5

Family Touring

Once you have made the decision to take the family on the Kangaroo Route, it may be worth making a list of good things to do while you narrow your destinations.

Some of these places have been mentioned in other parts of the book, others may be more worthwhile from a child's perspective than an adult one. Places here include zoos, sanctuaries, adventure and theme parks, historical sights and particular playgrounds.

For those not driving in Oz, bus tours are available to most of the major sights mentioned.

Just a reminder, especially for families traveling during the summer. Bring water bottles, juice packs and/or your insulated bag (the one you had on the plane) on your day trips, along with your hats, sunglasses and sunblock. Even when you travel away from the beaches, you must remember the sun is stronger here than it is in southern Florida or California. Protect yourselves.

Aussie Animals to See and Touch

One of the biggest attractions to Australia for many people remains the unique wildlife, caused by isolation of the Australian continent. Every continent, subcontinent, rain forest and ecosystem house its own flora and fauna, but none have received the attention Australian marsupials do (short of the Chinese panda).

Many go Down Under to see koalas and kangaroos. Few visitors realize there number more than 100 marsupials or pouched non-placental mammals who make their home somewhere in the Australian territory. The Aussies take their pouched friends for granted, spotting them in the gardens or the trees around the house. Some marsupials are considered pests. Like squirrels in the attic, possums can wreak havoc in the roof. Most foreigners would be surprised to learn there are 45 different kinds of kangaroos.

The other famous Aussie recognized around the world is the platypus. This furry little mammal is not a marsupial but a monotreme, cousin to the echidna, Australia's spiny anteater. These are the world's only two species of mammals which lay eggs, not live young. Amazing little creatures, they date back to prehistoric forms of Mammalia.

On the seal of Australia, the kangaroo faces an emu, a tall ostrich-like flightless bird. These dull brown birds can be seen grazing in flocks like their four-footed friends in the dusty Australian bush. On the other extreme, another flightless bird for which Australia has become known is the fairy penguin. Only about a foot tall, the tiny fish-eater makes its home along the Southern Ocean coast. The most accessible rookery is at Phillip Island a few hours from Melbourne.

Some of the world's most sought-after tropical birds are native to Australia: the sulphur-crested cockatoo, the smaller cockatiel, a number of colorful parrots and the little budgerigar, commonly called a budgie in your local pet shop.

Australia has only one wild dog, the dingo, a ferocious carnivore most common in outback regions. The tan-colored canine sits on par with a coyote or wolf.

Lizards of all kinds make their home in Australia. The large monitor has kept its aboriginal name, **goanna**. Crocodiles abound in the waters of the tropical north. Both saltwater and freshwater crocs remain abundant.

In the ocean, the variety and splendor of reef fish is unmatched anywhere in the world and so the ferocious denizens of the deep. The deadly sea snake and sea wasp (jellyfish) or **stinger** roam the warm waters. Sharks (known as **Noah's Arks** or **Noahs** in Aussie rhyming slang) remain a danger, carefully watched by Aussie surfers and swimmers.

Obviously, every unique animal cannot be described here. The traveler in Oz may have the opportunity to see others up close in their natural habitat.

As has been done in each section, these pages will take you around the continent pointing out a few places in each state that might be of interest particularly to families traveling Down Under. The list here will only include the easier ways to come in contact with wildlife. Adventurers visiting rain forests, the reef or taking advantage of farm stays and station stops will have additional opportunities not described here.

Remember Aussies love their outdoors, so plan to picnic wherever you go. It would be rare not to find clean picnic and barbecue areas and **ablution blocks** (bathrooms) in parks, zoos and sanctuaries.

Queensland

Queensland covers a huge territory, from the rain forests of the Far North to the metropolitan area of Brisbane, the state's capital city. Day trips from major points allow great chances to see and touch wildlife.

Outside the capital city of Brisbane sits one of Australia's premier petting parks. **Lone Pine Koala Sanctuary** houses koalas in close proximity and allows paid-for photos of humans posing with a koala. (Scientific studies on koalas, their habitats and their illnesses have been conducted here.) But even more fun, you can walk through herds of tame kangaroos, wallabies and meet some emus, too. A sanctuary like this may be your best chance to pose with a kanga or two. The large collection of native birds and other Aussie animals, including the Tasmanian devil and dingoes, can be viewed in outdoor pens. An outdoor aviary lets you see close up the large flying foxes, one of the world's largest species of bat. Lone Pine is a short drive (7 miles SW) into the outer suburb of **Fig Tree Pocket** but can also be reached by a lovely boat trip on the Brisbane River from the city. The Queensland information office in the city can tell you times and starting points. It's a great place to picnic and they have a kiosk with outdoor tables and basic Aussie **takeaway**.

One reservation about Lone Pine in recent years is that bus tours have made an otherwise small place overcrowded at times. The walking paths are not suited for big crowds and that one photo of you and the koala could mean a long **queue**.

Brisbanites sometimes suggest a trip to **Alma Park Zoo and Tropical Park Gardens**, en route from Brisbane north to the **Sunshine Coast**. It offers a chance to meet the Aussies as well as bushwalk through a tropical landscape. If your trip takes you toward the **Gold Coast**, you might make a stop at **Currumbin Sanctuary**, 11 miles south of **Surfers Paradise**. What was once only a bird sanctuary, known for its flocks of beautiful rainbow lorikeets, has now become a showcase for animals as well.

All three charge entrance fees which are quite steep; ask about family passes.

If you plan to stay in Brisbane for a few days, you might like to look into the **Australian Woolshed** at **Ferny Hills**, 9 miles north. It offers sheep-shearing, wool-spinning and sheep-dog demonstrations. A sheep show may be on the agenda. Other animals can be viewed in outdoor pens and the gift shop houses a fine selection of Australian arts and crafts.

Walkabout Creek offers a look at life in a **billabong**. The children's center shows terrariums of life beneath the surface. Above it all, raised decks allow stunning views of the Australian bush and a huge reservoir. At the top sits an indoor/outdoor cafe, great for morning tea or lunch in the eucalyptus-scented treetops.

On the **Sunshine Coast**, an hour-and-a-half north of Brisbane, our suggestion for a rotten day outdoors is to spend it indoors at **Underwater World** at Mooloolaba. Billed as Australia's largest tropical oceanarium, it offers a shark tank, a marvelous "touch" tank, outdoor seal pools and an ocean adventure movie. But the biggest attraction is the undersea tunnel. You stand on the people conveyor, or walk if you like, under an ocean of sea creatures. From reef to the deep, you find yourself beneath sharks, turtles, schools of colorful tropical fish and giant gropers. Even the smallest child is mesmerized by the experience. And, you can go through as many times as you like!

The oceanarium has been built as part of the **Wharf at Mooloolaba** complex. Boutiques, restaurants and ice cream shops line the waterfront on the spit and one courtyard features a terrific little maze-style playground. I warn you, once the kids get in, they may not want to come out. The adults in our group took turns watching the kids while the others browsed.

For those traveling in and around the Great Barrier Reef region and the city of **Townsville**, you'll have a chance of not only getting out on the Reef, but to observe it in an aquarium setting. The **Great Barrier Reef**

Wonderland rivals the oceanarium at Mooloolaba with an undersea tunnel and what's billed as the world's largest living coral reef aquarium.

Billabong Sanctuary will give you a chance to meet a collection of Australia's land animals including crocodiles, kangaroos and wombats.

New South Wales

In cosmopolitan **Sydney**, two terrific opportunities to meet the feathers, fur and fins of Australia exist in extremely beautiful settings: **Taronga Park Zoo** and **Sydney Aquarium**.

The zoo can be reached by ferry from Circular Quay to the landing at **Mosman** across the harbour. A large collection of Australian animals coexist with an international collection, equalling more than 3,500 animals. In the nocturnal house you witness many of the marsupials, who come out at night, like the lumbering wombat, and many varieties of marsupial mice. The zoo offers children's strollers free of charge. Open every day.

The biggest treat remains the spectacular panorama of the harbor which can be seen from within the zoo. Even non-zoo people enjoy a walk and a picnic in this phenomenal park setting. A small aquarium was once housed at the zoo, but in the 1980s, a new aquarium was constructed as part of the **Darling Harbour** development. The marine life display includes 12-foot-long saltwater crocodiles. But as stated in the Queensland section, the best thing about the modern aquariums in Australia have to be the undersea tunnels—the Sydney Aquarium has two! While the entry fees are steep, they are something the whole family will really enjoy.

The Darling Harbour complex houses a mall area, food court and entertainment both day and evening.

North of the city lies **Koala Park Sanctuary** where you can cuddle a koala and have your picture taken. Other animals include dingoes, kangas and wallaroos.

Emus wander about as well. Several other kanga/koala sites include: **Australian** (at **Eastern Creek**), **Waratah** (at **Terry Hills**) and **Featherdale** (at **Doonside**) wildlife parks.

To meet domestic animals, head for the **Blue Mountains** and the **Megalong Valley Farm.** This real-life sheep and cattle station offers working demonstrations and animal displays on weekends. Barnyard petting can be found in the little section called Friendship Farm. Admission is reasonable.

Another farm visit 40 miles (64 km) north of Sydney is **Tobruk Merino Sheep Farm**, set on the ridges of the Hawkesbury River. Merinos remain Australia's finest wool sheep and their fleeces are sought all over the world. Tobruk offers a working woolshed with various demonstrations.

The North Coast of N.S.W. remains a good stopping point for long-distance travelers. At **Coffs Harbour**, the kids can take in the **Pet Porpoise Pool** with its 90-minute sea circus and a giant aquarium housing sharks, reef fish, turtles and dolphins.

Canberra

Remember for a moment that Canberra remains landlocked—the only major Australian city not near the ocean. But Canberra is still the capital of this great island and will not be outdone by its seaside cousins. As you have been reading, you have been introduced to a few aquariums with fascinating undersea tunnels. Canberra hosts one too, the **National Aquarium**, complete with a collection of sharks and rays which can be very daunting when you find yourself beneath them. If your Canberra tour is your only chance at viewing an underwater tunnel, don't miss it; but if you can get to an oceanarium in a seaside location, you might enjoy it more.

Rehwinkle's Animal Park, 15 miles (24 km) north of

Canberra, offers a look at the fauna which roam *terra firma.* Birds and native bush creatures can be found in their natural habitats.

Real bushwalking with a chance to see Aussie animals can be done in the hills surrounding Canberra. The **Tidbinbilla Nature Reserve** sits 25 miles (40 km) southwest of the city and covers 12 thousand acres.

Victoria

In and around **Melbourne**, the capital, several opportunities exist to touch and view Aussie animals. The **Royal Melbourne Zoological Gardens** is considered the world's third oldest zoo. The garden setting makes for a beautiful outing. While Australian animals are featured, many international species make up the collection of 350 representatives. One unique display is the Butterfly House, featuring butterflies in a rain forest cohabiting with beautiful tropical birds. The Bushland Exhibit and the Great Flight Aviary expand the opportunities for visitors to bushwalk and meet Aussies first hand. Open every day.

To see an exclusively Aussie collection of 200 species of mammals, reptiles and birds, take a 45-minute drive to **Healesville Sanctuary** in the Dandenong Ranges east of Melbourne. It offers a wonderful chance to experience the bushland. The sanctuary breeds some of Australia's endangered and "threatened" (not-quite endangered) species. A rare potoroo and pygmy possum can be found in the Animals of the Night exhibition. Herds of kangaroos and wallabies roam through the paddocks alongside visitors. Open every day.

While you might get a chance to see kangaroos hopping through roadside paddocks or spot a koala in a eucalyptus tree, only one natural setting exists in which to witness little Aussies everyday like clockwork. It's the "penguin parade" of fairy penguins. A colony of the little penguins makes their home on **Phillip Island**, a couple of hours from Melbourne in coastal Gippsland. Every night at sunset, the public is welcomed on Summerland Beach in the **Phillip Island Penguin Reserve** to watch the foot-tall penguins returning home from their day of fishing. With each wave comes a flock of wet navy-blue birds. They shuffle up the beach looking for their burrows. The birds roam freely while the people stand in pens or watch from a grandstand. It's quite a remarkable sight. Bus tours and optional overnights can be arranged on Phillip Island, a local holiday spot for Victorians. A family can fill a whole day with nature activities at the Reserve, including displays at the Visitors Centre which reveal the undersea world of the fairy penguins.

If you plan to make this unforgettable highlight part of your visit during the summer, then organize the tour and tickets as soon as you arrive in Victoria. Any tourist agent can help. The penguins rate as Victoria's number-one tourist attraction. If you go off season, the nights get cool. Plan to "rug up," wearing jackets and hats and even bring a Thermos of coffee or hot chocolate for the kids.

Ballarat Wildlife and Reptile Park can be visited in conjunction with other sites in this historic city 70 miles (112 km) northwest of Victoria.

Tasmania

Tassie is known for good bushwalking among the island's beautiful flora and fauna. Bicycling remains a common mode of travel (as in America's New England region). But the biggest wildlife draw to this tiniest of states must be the "Tasmanian devil." Kids especially want to find the devil. They either picture a devilish looking animal or the American cartoon character bearing the same moniker. This marsupial carnivore looks nothing like its animated relative. Instead, the tiny black straight-furred animal could be mistaken for a cross between small feral dogs and cats. In the wild, it's almost impossible to find but wildlife parks house some devils for tourists to catch a fleeting glance of the jittery little animal.

Three places listed by the Australian Tourist Commission include **Tasmanian Devil Park** near Port Arthur, **Tasmanian Wildlife Park** 50 miles (80 km) west of Launceston, and **Bonorong Wildlife Park**, in Brighton, 16 miles (25 km) north of Hobart.

South Australia

Not to be outdone, the city of Adelaide has it own zoo. Fifteen hundred native and international birds and mammals complete the collection. If your trip must be limited to South Australia, take advantage of this beautiful zoo.

If you and your family are destined to meet and greet the marine mammals of Australia, **Kangaroo Island** may be just the place. The island is accessible by ferry only but can be a memorable sidetrip. During January (summer), the National Parks and Wildlife Service introduces children to the wonders of the island, including watching fairy penguins waddle along the beach from their long day fishing in the Southern Ocean.

For those who will find Australia's sea lions wonderful to look at and almost meet, Kangaroo Island offers the chance to view the huge animals lying on the beach, sunning or feeding their babies. The place is the **Seal Bay Conservation Park**, and walks near the colony must be guided by a park ranger.

Guided bushwalks in other reserves on the island will offer good closeups of other Aussie natives in their natural habitat.

Overnight accommodation can be obtained on the island but not cheaply.

Western Australia

Since Western Australia is so far from the rest of the country, the Perth area has some of the same major attractions as other parts of the country.

Here, too, is an **Underwater World** (See Queensland for full description), a modern aquarium with an undersea tunnel in which to view 5,000 varieties of marine life.

And to get the customary cuddle with a koala, the **Cohunu Wildlife Park** at **Gosnells** will be pleased to organize a photo opportunity for you. Cohunu has what's touted as the largest aviary in the Southern Hemisphere and areas filled with many other Aussie natives.

Western Australia offers one other unique animal attraction that no family would ever forget. However, it's off the beaten track and will take some planning to get there. The place is called **Monkey Mia** at **Shark Bay**, 400 miles (640 km) north of Perth. What's so special? Here you can actually feed and pet a school of wild dolphins! That's right, you just wade in, offer them some fish and they'll let you give them a rub. Because they are wild, the school leaves the area sometimes between November and April. So it's best to call ahead to the Shark Bay Visitor and Travel Centre before planning to go during those months. Shark Bay can be reached by plane or bus tours from Perth. This section of the west coast is well-known for good fishing as well.

Northern Territory

If you take your family as far as the N.T., you probably have interests in the Outback extremes. The Outback section describes excursions which will include Aussie animals.

Early Australia for Kids

Australian resort areas host many varieties of theme parks with thrill rides, water slides and kiddie amusements. They advertise heavily and are easy to find. For me, those kinds of adventure parks are not worth planning a trip around. If there is one in the area you are in and the kids need a diversion, then pick one.

Instead of spending time on the so-called theme parks, enjoy the alternatives. Historic recreations will not only be fun but will give your whole family a look at how Australia came to be. As elsewhere within this book, price of admission is not specifically given, just noted that it exists.

Sovereign Hill

In the state of **Victoria**, the Gold Rush years of the 1850s hold a special place in history. Life in that era comes alive at **Ballarat**. The city can be a long day trip or a pleasant overnight from Melbourne. Today, **Sovereign Hill,** an historical theme park, brings back life in that era better than any other place in Australia. Just 70 miles (112 km) outside the city center of Melbourne is the Diggings, where the Chinese Village for laborers and the homes and businesses of the township come alive like Brigadoon, stuck in the decade between 1851 and 1861. From 1861 to 1916 a more "modern" gold mine took the place of the earlier diggings. Guided tours and coach rides inform visitors on the finer points of history. There's plenty of period shops to browse and places to eat to pack a day with fun. The Gold Museum completes the tour. Admission with an optional two-day pass includes other sites in Ballarat.

Coal Creek

Mining for coal was also the basis of Victoria's economy, and a smaller re-creation at **Coal Creek**, two hours southeast of Melbourne in the Gippsland district, offers a wonderful look at a coal mining town of the last century. This park was lovingly created by residents of the district and offers a warmth which other more commercial sites could never match. Rides on a horse-pulled dray and afternoon tea of homemade scones and cream can complete the visit. Admission fees.

Fitzroy Gardens

In Melbourne proper, the actual house of Captain Cook is located in Fitzroy Gardens (shipped piece by piece from its original site in England). It's a cute curiosity for the family. To make the visit complete, a kid-sized Tudor village has been constructed nearby.

Old Melbourne Gaol

Near Melbourne's present-day police headquarters at Russell Street, goal exhibits include some of infamous and legendary bushranger Ned Kelly's belongings. The Gaol shows a bit of the history from Melbourne's penal past.

Other Gaols

Sydney has an Old Gaol exhibit as well as Perth, South Australia and several towns in Tasmania which were once the worst of the penal colonies. (See City-by-City, Chapter 2.)

Old Sydney Town

Now that we are in N.S.W., look for **Old Sydney Town**, another town restoration. The township is at **Somersby**, near **Gosford**, about two hours north of Sydney. (This area was affected by hugh bushfires in January 1994.) Sydneytown recreates the penal days of Sydney, with colonial crafts exhibits and period buildings. Sometimes the town square holds a flogging or two. Most people say, it only takes a few hours to experience everything. Admission fees.

Timbertown

On N.S.W. North Coast, Timbertown is at **Wauchope**

near **Port Macquarie**. The sign reads "Welcome to the carefree days of 1880." I don't know how carefree those days were, but Timbertown introduces the visitor to a re-creation of "Bushcamp" life, reliant on the tall trees of N.S.W. A working sawmill and period craftshops show the kids how it used to be. If your trip takes you along this part of the coast north of Sydney, Timbertown may be a good alternative to a day at the beach. Admission fees.

Historic Transportation

For Train Enthusiasts

A number of small-gauge historical trains have been restored around Australia for tourist runs. At **Victor Harbour**, south of Adelaide on the Fleurieu Peninsula, the **Cockle Train** steams over a scenic 30-minute ride along the ocean on Australia's oldest public railway. The town was founded as a whaling site. Another famous trip is on ***Puffing Billy*** in the **Dandenong Ranges** in Victoria. You can spend the day riding Puffing Billy through the mountain towns, or get off for a picnic and swim and rejoin the train. You can even take the train to get to Puffing Billy. The commuter train from Melbourne's Flinders Street Station takes passengers to **Belgrave**, 70 minutes from the city, where they can connect with the steam train. Special holiday events, luncheon tours and evening rides are scheduled. The **Steam Museum** is at **Menzies Creek**, one of the stops along the way.

For Water Buffs

The town of **Echuca**, Victoria, is perhaps the most famous of the river towns. **Paddlesteamers** ply the river near the restored wharf for tourist trips. The little main street was refurbished as the setting for a television series called *All the Rivers Run*. Echuca is not a park but a modern town complemented by its historic areas. Kids love the big-wheeled boats and the long steps down the wharves.

At **Fremantle**, sits a full-scale model of the *Endeavour*, the ship in which Captain Cook sailed to Australia and claimed the land for England. Artisans using 18th-century methods are crafting the ship in place at dockside.

Part II

Aussie Words

Chapter 6

Aussie Speaking

"**G'day, Mate**," one man says to another as he gets off the plane in Melbourne (pronounced *Mel-bun*), Australia. "Do you have plans for the weekend? Maybe you'd like to join us for the **footy** on Saturday **arvo**. We usually leave early to get in the **car park** at the **M.C.G.** and then we get a good **possie**, split open some **tinnies** from the **esky** and have a few **sangers** before the match."

If the newcomer is a **Yank** then he's going to need some help with this conversation. No one's trying to be **cheeky**. Aussies talk this way. Between the Aussie accent and the words slung together without a break, it's easy to get lost.

Here's some help for this situation:

G'day, Mate — greeting between men
Footy — Australian Rules Football
Arvo — afternoon (a contraction of sorts)
Car Park — parking lot
M.C.G. — Melbourne Cricket Ground
Possie — position (spot, space or seat)
Tinnies — Tin (or aluminum) cans of beer
Esky — ice chest (from a brand name)
Sangers — sandwiches
Yank — American
Cheeky — jokingly sarcastic

If you think this is just sports jargon and these words don't really exist, be assured they do. They are part of the everyday English of Australia. While the English spoken in Australia and the version spoken in America originate in Mother England, the development of the languages in the last two hundred years took divergent turns. Today, they remain as much different as they are alike.

In Australia, The Queen's English has been recreated by a colorful people who cultivated new words to describe unusual animals, birds and plants, home-grown household and farm articles, work and play. The isolation of the people became a fertile field for seedlings of an old tongue to blossom into a cross-pollinated hybrid.

Some people refer colloquially to Australian-English as **strine**. Others argue that strine is not actually the spoken language. It is more the sound of the words as they run together quickly, under-enunciated by a partially closed mouth and salted with a nasal tone. For example: "Didya'avagoodweekend?" translates to "Did you have a good weekend? "Not everyone speaks this way but many do. Others use strine as the umbrella for Aussie slang only. Whatever way you understand strine, the word should be included in your Aussie nomenclature, but, since there is no consensus, this book will continue to call the language Aussie-English, not strine.

Clipped Words

To comprehend the colloquial differences, we must understand the basics of how the Aussie mind thinks. The fundamental rule is: **If the word is long—perhaps two syllables or more—clip it and add a *y* sound!**

Perhaps the simplest and most obvious example of this is the word *Australians*. Along with the rest of the world, citizens of the Lucky Country call themselves **Aussies**, pronounced with a *zee-zee* sound.

We've already seen a few examples of this "clip-it-plus-y" syndrome in our sample conversation. **Tinnies** comes from tin-cans-of-beer shortened to tin cans and turned into tinnies. The game of Australian Rules Football or **Aussie Rules**—not soccer, not rugby—is never called by its real name in Melbourne, the country's footy capital. **Melburnians** say **footy** and that's that!

From the moment Australians get up in the morning, they start clipping words. They've deemed the first meal of the day **brekky**, when they may have tea with **bickies**, otherwise known as **biscuits**, which are really crackers or cookies. (That will be explained further in the food chapter.) Newspapers have even featured listings for "The Best Brekky in Town." To New Yorkers, it rivals an early brunch!

Even the holidays are not sacred when it comes to language. In general, Aussies refer to the Christmas season as **the hollies**. Smack in the middle of the summer, Christmas seems to have lost its formality. Many people retreat to their **holly house** for **Chrissy** since this is the big getaway time of year. The kids have **hollies** from school and most folks take their long **holiday** from work. Vacations do not exist in the nomenclature. Children look forward to **Chrissy** like kids the world over, hoping to get **prezzies** from **Father Christmas**.

These are probably enough examples to give you an

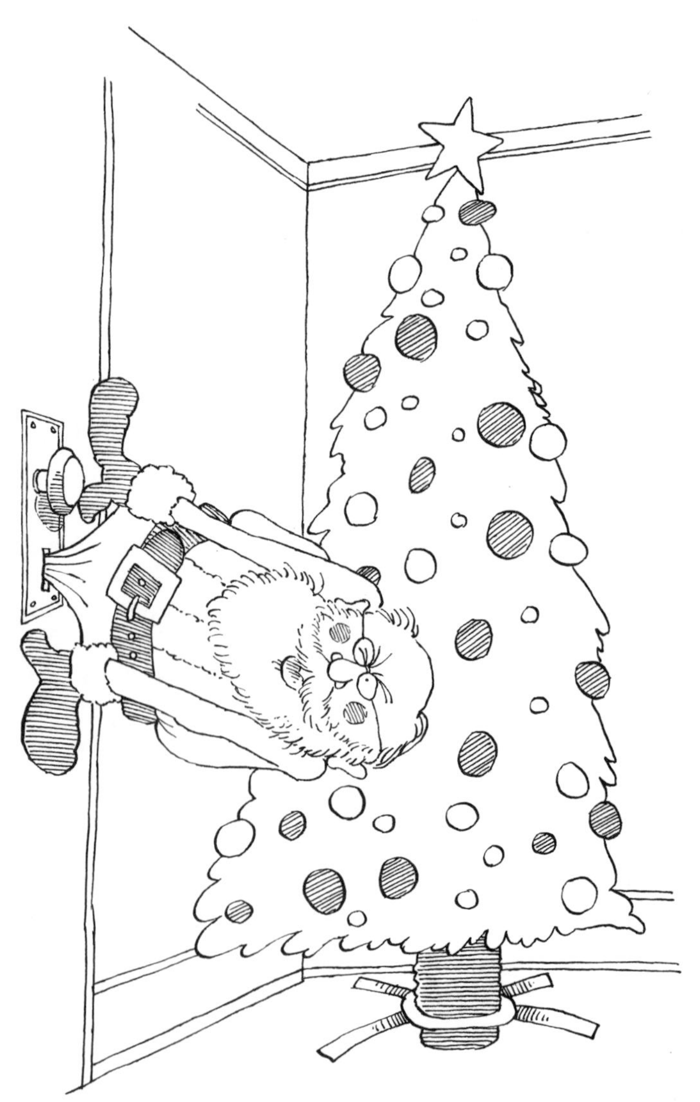

"father christmas" comes in through the keyhole!

idea what we mean about "**clip-it-plus-*y***" but in the following chapters you'll learn more about the specific uses of shortened words which describe occupations, school days, things in the house, the car and its parts.

Rhyming Slang

The second colorful derivation of the Queen's English employed Down Under is **rhyming slang**. The cockney convicts transported to the 18th-century penal colony, which would become the country of Australia, brought with them this barbarism of the spoken tongue. The cockneyisms are not used constantly but they do slip into conversations often enough to merit explanation. It should be noted that Aussies wholeheartedly adopted the practice of creating descriptive rhymes and from them developed new phrases no cockney could recognize.

Here's a sample dialogue to give your ear a chance to hear what is being explained. Read it aloud and see if it makes sense to you.

A husband is telling his mate about taking holidays:

"Me and the **cheese and kisses** are taking the **billy lids** off to **Steak and Kidney** in the morning. We're leaving right after we take our morning **plastic flower** and drop the **hollow log** with the neighbours."

Are you wondering what this conversation means? See if you can make sense of it using the following rhymes:

Cheese and kisses rhymes with "Mrs." (The Mrs.).

Billy lids rhymes with "kids" (children).

Steak and Kidney rhymes with Sydney (the Australian city).

Plastic flower rhymes with shower.

Hollow log rhymes with dog.

The complete translation reads as follows:

"My wife and I are taking the children to Sydney in the morning. We're leaving right after we take our morning showers and drop the dog with our neighbors."

This small sampling represents only a portion of the combinations spoken throughout Oz. Ready for more?

The family monikers do not end here. **Trouble and**

strife doubles for **cheese and kisses** because the last word of the phrase rhymes with wife. **China plate** then becomes mate or spouse. While **billy lids** were defined as kids, you probably don't know that a billy lid is a pot cover, because billy is a pot in which to boil water (more about those definitions later).

The **hollow log** chases the **Ballarat**. In this case, a place name becomes the rhyme. Ballarat is a rural city in the state of Victoria, not far from Melbourne. An **Oxford scholar** is not a person. **Scholar** rhymes with dollar.

The phrase **Warwick Farms** (a suburb of Sydney, pronounced WAR-rick) substitutes for arms, which rhymes with farms; and **Under the Warwick Farms** has come to mean underarms. You may have noted that once the rhymes themselves become familiar they too get shortened. **Oxford** will mean dollar and **under the Warwicks** will denote underarms. The Aussies can get carried away. From these colorful phrases euphemisms grow. **Trouble under the Warwicks** means it is time for a **plastic** (the shortened version of **plastic flower** or shower).

Pick up the Al Capone or **answer the eau de cologne** both tell you to answer the phone. If you are told to wear a **bag of fruit** for a dinner party, don't be insulted. Your host requests you wear a suit. And if you would like to top it off properly, you'll don a **tit-for-tat**, or commonly called a **tit-for**. Remember the rules and you'll realize **tat** rhymes with hat and you'll be all set.

When taking a **Captain Cook** you simply take a look, but a **babbling brook** stands for cook. How does a layman know which is which? Practice. Aussies will say you learn the meanings and commit them to memory like the alphabet or any other vocabulary.

Sometimes in rhyming slang the context changes the meaning. Just as Captain Cook and Al Capone have gotten into the act, so has **Bob Hope**. This comedian takes the place of either soap or dope (as in drugs). I wonder if Mr. Hope knows that? Sometimes **Bob Hope** will be found soaking beneath a **plastic flower**; but at other times the people who deal or abuse **Bob Hope** may run into **John Hop**. He's the guy on the beat, dressed in blue, ready to throw the **crim** (criminal) into the **divvy van** and drive away. The **divvy van** belongs to the divisional police headquarters (similar to a precinct) and is the equivalent of a paddy wagon. (Of course, paddy wagon is considered U.S. slang, a phrase with its own colorful history.)

If you run away from **the johns** (the pared version of **John Hops** or cops) you'll be going it **Pat Malone**—going alone! Because of this meaning, john is not synonymous with toilet.

Words of a Different Colour

To add to the minor difficulties you may already be having, quite a few words in Aussie-English are the same as in American-English but the pronunciations vary slightly (even if the accents are the same). It may take a moment for an American ear to catch up with the spoken word. Anyone familiar with British-English will find some variations easy enough to comprehend. Most of them were born as old English forms, dropped by Americans generations ago.

Some examples will provide you with some understanding: Horseracing tops the list as Australia's number one spectator sport, a true national pastime rivaled only by cricket. A big race is called a derby, just like in the U.S. but it's pronounced *darby*. The *e* is pronounced like an *a*. The word clerk follows the same rule. The *clark* will help you now.

American trains attempt to run on or close to schedule. The word contains a *sked* sound. But the Aussies talk about train schedules with a soft *shed* sound. No one will ever ask for a train sked. Another familiar word which sounds different is jaguar. While the American name of the animal has only two syllables, the Aussies lengthened the sound to *Jag-gu-aahr*. Perhaps that makes the luxury car more luxurious and the great cat more sleek.

A favorite word that causes a bit of consternation is aluminum. The British and the Australians say *Al-u-min-ee-um*. That's because they go one step further here and spell the word with an extra syllable: **aluminium.** See the *mini* there! The American word does not contain that syllable. By the way, the stuff housekeepers wrap the leftovers in has been reduced to **al-foil**—fewer syllables all the way around.

Tyres on the car, **colour**, **flavour**, **favour**, **harbour** and **labour** keep the British spelling with a notable exception: **The Australian Labor Party (ALP)**—which is as big as the Republicans or Democrats. **The ALP** spells labor the American way. That's the equivalent of naming a product "lite" instead of "light."

When parking a car in Australia, a driver might be surprised when his **tyres** rub the **kerb** until he reads a construction sign explaining: **Kerb Realignment in Process.** That means the local **council** (town, village or county government—whoever is in charge) has decided to narrow the road to slow leadfooted drivers.

Australians employ many other Britishisms constantly throughout their language, too many to name them all. But, let's look at a few more everyday terms which will be familiar to your ear but not your eye.

Cheque, as in traveler's cheque or bank cheque is not a fancier way to spell check. Instead, **cheque** is the correct and only spelling for the monetary substitution in the Queen's English and the banking system run by her subjects. Check is strictly American. Another example of a "sound alike" can be found in the elongated version of **tonne**. It seems like a ton of letters to use for a monosyllabic word, but the Aussies use it to denote the metric **tonne**, which weighs more than the U.S. ton.

If you are expecting a package during your visit Down Under, you may have to pick it up at the shipping company's **despatch** office. Do not let it throw you. They will dispatch the parcel anyway, you hope.

With these basics, most English speaking people should start to comprehend and feel comfortable with the fresh and, in many cases, witty words, expressions and euphemisms which have evolved from the workaday world of **The Antipodes**. Ah, there's another surname for Australia which you may have heard but do not understand. **Antipodes** is the early mapmakers' reference to Australia, used by the British to describe their colony in the Southern Hemisphere. *Antipodes* stems from the Greek, meaning on the opposite side of the globe.

Summary & Reminders

When you first set foot on **Terra Australis**, keep in mind shortened words can describe anything—clothing, travel destinations, food, drink or sports—as can rhyming slang. The idioms weave in and out of conversations between mother and child, farmers and white-collar workers, and can be heard on television and radio broadcasts. The **pollies** rely on colloquialisms as much as the banker and **milk-o** do.

The Aussie tongue has few regionalisms. The only divisions in the spoken language are bits of jargon leaning more toward country life than life in the cities. But in a nation reliant on its farmers and graziers, and where agriculture still dominates most of the livable land, you will find country words easily understood. In some cases, they've been expanded to take on new citified definitions, but the original meanings are not lost.

Phrases which may seem outdated stay alive lovingly in the nation's ballads and poetry and get passed to each generation of children and visitors.

You may note spellings of the same word may differ in this text from other Australian publications and that various Australian texts will not agree either. Words like **milk-o** may appear as **milk-oh** (the shortened version of milkman). Both are correct. The clipped version of barbecue may be written **barby** or **barbie.** This copy generally follows **The Macquarie Dictionary**, whenever possible; but in some cases, two or more spellings have become acceptable and are listed as slang or jargon which have not found their way into serious dictionaries. In the end, they appear the way a writer's ear hears them.

Chapter 7

The Tucker Bag

What are submarine sandwiches called where you live? Hoagies? grinders? subs? heroes? wedges or po' boys? All of these different words from different regions of America describe the same things: two pieces of bread with food in the middle. Well, head's up! There are more names for sandwiches coined by Australians to describe their version of bread-on-the-outside-food-in-the-middle: **sanger** is the most common and **jaffle** has its own place in the kitchen!

They say, food is the universal language—but not if you have to ask for it by name. Everyone eats. But food is personal, protected by pet names in every country. The kind of food, how it is prepared and how it is eaten reflects the nation's lifestyle and standard of living, as well as climate, history and tradition.

Australia is no different.

Here Bruce and his mate are talking over a **cuppa** during **morning tea:**

Bruce: "The **cheese and kisses** made some great **tucker** for **tea** last night. A bit of **snags** in the **griller** along with nice fresh **pumpkin.** It was just right!"

Mate: "I can't even think about last night, I'm **full as a goog** from **brekky**. I stopped in that new **coffee lounge** and had **spags on toast** with the **billy lids**. They took so long to finish, I filled up on **crumpets** and **jam**. The

littlies like to eat out. But what they eat! **Beans on toast** is fine, but with **lemon squash** at eight o'clock in the morning!

Bruce: "My kids would rather eat that than **muesli** any day! Y'know, my wife packs them a **tuckerbag** for school lunch with **Vegemite** or **beetroot sangers** but she swears they don't eat it. Instead, they go to the **tuckshop** and fill up on **lollies** and **bickies**. That's going to stop!"

Lost? There are a few Aussie words in this conversation that were introduced before and some will not show up for another chapter or two but most of the new words found in this dialog describe something edible or food related.

Morning tea: equivalent of the a.m. coffee break

Cheese and kisses: Not edible. Mrs., wife (rhyming slang)

Tucker: everyday food

Tea: evening meal, supper, dinner

Snags: sausages

Griller: broiler section of your stove

Pumpkin: not what you're thinking—this is squash!

Full as a goog: stuffed

Goog: an egg

Brekky: breakfast

Coffee Lounge: coffee shop, cafe

Spags on toast: canned spaghetti in sauce piled on toast

Billy lids: kids (rhyming slang)

Crumpets: similar to English muffins but not exactly.

Jam: never jelly

Beans on toast: canned baked beans on toast, a breakfast food.

Lemon Squash: pulpy lemon soda.

Muesli: a kind of breakfast granola/European style.

Tuckerbag: a bag to put food in

Vegemite: a brand name for a spread, as common as peanut butter.

Beetroot: red beets, commonly sliced on sandwiches.

Tuckshop: school snack bar

Lollies: candy

Bickies: cookies or crackers

This is just a sampling of fare but a few more heaping helpings are on the way.

Generally, when you talk about food in Australia, you talk about **tucker**. Whether you are asked: "Will you stay for tucker?" or hear a television commercial touting a brand of macaroni as "Good Aussie Tucker!" the word will not escape you. **Tucker** fills the market shelves, Mum's kitchen and the **takeaway shop**. No gourmet frills here.

Historically, **tucker** was carried on a wagon stored in a **tuckerbox**, an early version of a cooler. But if a man traveled on foot or horseback, he carried his lunch in a **tuckerbag**. Now, there's a chain of supermarkets called Tuckerbag. Very clever!

A **tuckshop** sounds like something a tailor would run; but, Australian school children buy snacks or quick lunches at the school tuckshop. Mums even volunteer to staff the tuckshop, the equivalent of a snack bar.

Asked for a unique example of food Down Under most people would answer: **Vegemite**, probably followed by the **meat pie**. **Vegemite** is a black salty paste composed of yeast extract produced by Kraft, the cheese food company. Three generations of Australian mothers have been convinced that Vegemite is good for their children. They spread it thinly on toast or **dry bickies** and serve it for lunch, breakfast or snacks. Aussie kids ask for **Vegemite sangers** as often as American kids ask for peanut butter and jelly. The Vegemite jar label took on cult status similar to the place the Campbell's soup can found in pop art. It shows up on beach towels, puzzles, posters and greeting cards.

Somewhere in your travels, you may hear the comparative expression: It's as **dinky-di Aussie as Vegemite**. That's about as Australian as you can get. The phrase is the equivalent of: As American as apple pie. **Dinky-di** substitutes for truly, honestly or true blue.

Some words of warning: If you were not weaned on Vegemite, you may never acquire a taste for it. Or worse, you might never get past the smell!

Already, you have come across the word **brekky** for breakfast, but now let us elaborate on what people eat in the morning. You may have a **cuppa** of **white tea** or **white coffee** or even black tea or coffee. But, if you order it **white** be prepared to have it served with the milk already mixed in—and lots of milk at that! If you do not care for it so milky, ask for black with milk or cream on the side.

Other than Vegemite on toast, **jam** is another option but jelly isn't. In Australia, **jelly** is the clipped version of gelatin (like JELL-O).

Pikelets may be on the menu. They are fat, doughy silver-dollar-size pancakes. Maple syrup will not arrive on the table with them since maple trees are not indigenous to Australia. Actually, maple syrup has started to show up on supermarket shelves but many Australians think of it as a dessert topping. They have their own sweet breakfast topping, **golden syrup** or **treacle**, made during the processing of sugar cane. Cane farming is big business in Australia, so it is almost patriotic to choose treacle over an American import.

Aussies enjoy dry cereals, too. Afterall, they grow acres and acres of wheat and other grains. Commercially-marketed cereals bear similar names to their American cousins but one popular brand does not ring true: Kellogg's Rice Krispies are **Rice Bubbles**.

Often a motel will provide tea or coffee and **sweet biscuits** or **sweet bickies** for a quick brekky. Do not think of biscuits as the dinner rolls Americans butter. **Sweet biscuits** come out of a cookie bag and **dry bickies** mean saltines and their relatives. Cookies only became commonly known in Australia after Beaver started eating cookies and milk on Aussie television and the Cookie Monster moved onto Sesame Street in Sydney.

Aussies like English muffins but they request **crumpets** more often. Both fit in toasters and go well with butter and other spreads but they taste different. Try them. Baked goods like blueberry muffins or corn muffins can be found, but you will not hear them called muffins. Sometimes bakers refer to them as breakfast cakes or little cakes.

Tea, Tea or Tea?

Scones look and taste like American biscuits. A hostess usually offers scones for **morning tea** or **afternoon tea**. Both of these rituals follow British tradition. Work stops for these breaks, so do school and sporting events.

Australians sometimes enjoy a more festive British **Devonshire tea** as well, around three or four in the afternoon, sometimes called high tea in England. The **Devvy tea** seems incongruous with most of the Australian climate. Usually this tea is offered in the afternoon—a pot of tea and scones served with heavy whipped cream and jam. Lusciously sweet! What a treat, but not at 100 degrees Fahrenheit! Driving through the Queensland countryside, sweltering in the sun does not seem the time to stop for hot tea and warm biscuits, but you may see a sign for **tea rooms**. Stop the car. Try it. You may never do it again!

In that blistering heat, under which most of Australia suffers, an American might look for a tall frosty iced tea to quench his thirst. He can search all he wants. He probably will never find it; and he'll get some strange looks along the way. I once got a cup of hot tea when I asked for iced tea. I thought the waitress just did not understand correctly. So, unknowingly, I asked again for iced tea. She thought I meant ice in my tea. The next thing I knew, a saucer of ice cubes was plunked down beside my teacup and the waitress walked away mumbling something unflattering under her breath. My traveling companion looked at me like I was the crazy one! Even when I tried to explain the look remained quizzical.

I must admit I did find instant tea once in a supermarket gourmet section which had directions for making iced tea on the dusty container, but I doubt if any Aussie shoppers read the label. Even if they did, they would not take it seriously.

Do not despair totally. You will find **iced coffee**, but

it may surprise you. At first glance on a menu, the price may catch you off guard—much higher than you would expect to pay for cold coffee with ice in it. But you think, I'm thirsty. Price doesn't matter. You order the iced coffee and, minutes later, this milkshake-sized glass arrives with whipped cream streaming over the side and you think, I didn't order that! But you did. The Oz version of iced coffee is a treat, a dessert almost, like a milkshake, ice cream soda or float. It starts out as coffee with lots of milk added, then the scoops of ice cream and a spiral of whipped cream on top! Granted, though it is lovely, it may not be what you had in mind. Enjoy it anyway. Afterall, you have come to Australia to have a good time, so what if it means a few extra calories.

Roadhouse Tucker

On breakfast menus in **roadhouses** (roadside diners) or **coffee lounges** (luncheonettes or coffee shops), two strange selections, which you read in our dialogues, may be found: **spaghetti or spags on toast** and **baked beans on toast**. Baked beans seldomly show up anywhere except breakfast. They come out of cans and are made with a tomato-based sauce rather than like Boston-style beans with molasses.

Sandwich nicknames were mentioned early in this chapter but now it is time to describe what a sandwich means. The mainstays for lunch stack more thinly than most American sandwiches. **Sangers** consist of a sliver of meat—maybe ham, fresh chicken pieces or **silverside** (similar to corned beef)—or a single slice of cheese or tomato; even a salad sandwich may be made with lettuce and thinly sliced **beetroot** (red beets). In an ethnically German area you might find the traditional German cold cuts as you would find Italian favorites in an Italian immigrant neighborhood, but you certainly will not find wide varieties in most supermarkets or convenience stores.

Mayonnaise can be found but not commonly. The Aussies consider mayo a salad dressing rather than a bread spread. Usually sanger makers spread a thick layer of butter, not margarine, on their **roses are red** (rhyming slang for bread). "So, butter up some **roses**, Mate!" may be heard in the kitchen around noon.

What should be emphasized is the diminutive size of these sandwiches. They are made with a sliver of food on them and maybe a piece of lettuce, then cut to resemble the little finger sandwiches Aunt Bea may have brought to the bridge club luncheon. This clarifies why someone will order a **plate of sangers** or a **plate of toasted sangers**. It takes a plateful to fill you.

A fancier kind of toasted sandwich is a **jaffle.** They

spaghetti on toast

butter a jaffle inside and out, put the food in the middle of the bread and place the whole thing between the hot plates of a **jaffle iron**. The jaffle iron works like a waffle iron. The heat toasts the bread and melts the contents, making a kind of grilled sandwich without the grill. When I first noticed these in Australia, I had not seen anything comparable in America, but sandwich makers are now an American kitchen appliance. How many of them hide in people pantries these days, I cannot say, but they still do not seem as popular as the Aussie jaffle.

The Milk Bar

For lunch on the run, or any other meal for that matter, **takeaway shops** abound—that's takeout under an assumed name. There you pick up some of the fast foods that helped shape the Aussie palate long before McDonald's and Kentucky Fried Chicken arrived. In addition to takeaway shops, hungry Australians stop at the **milk bar**. They consider milk bars a unique phenomenon but they are closely related to the old-fashioned corner store, bodega or mom-and-pop shop. Perhaps what sets a milk bar apart is the grill and deep fryer to make hamburgers and fish and **chips** (french fries).

As mentioned earlier, the Aussie-est of foods and certainly the premier takeaway treat is the **meat pie**, which equals a personal-size pot pie heated in a **pie warmer.** Traditionally, the pie maker fills his pies with ground **(minced)** beef and a spicy brown gravy. Non-traditional pies may be stuffed with minced lamb or just vegetables. No matter, Aussies eat **pies** covered in green peas (called a **pie-and-peas**) or smothered in **sauce.**

Sauce is ketchup, or catsup—short for **tomato sauce** (or **dead horse** in rhyming slang). Since tomato sauce comes out of a ketchup bottle, Aussies douse pasta with spaghetti sauce, red sauce or marinara sauce. Aussies like Worcestershire sauce but refer to it as **black sauce**, not to be confused with Chinese black bean sauce or soy sauce which looks black, too. Soy sauce hides behind a label marked **soya sauce.**

Chinese laborers came to Australia during the gold rush years in the mid-1800s. Some of their favorite foods were Australianized and adopted as takeaway fare: **Chiko rolls, spring rolls** and **dim sims.** Chiko and spring rolls both equal the Aussie version of egg rolls. **Chiko** denotes a brand name of frozen prepared snacks cooked for sale in most takeaways. **Dim sim** represents another mass-marketed delicacy. Bite-sized spicy meat wrapped in a thin dough creates the fast-food dim sim. You will usually find them fried and sometimes steamed. Chinese restaurants often advertise **dim sim lunches** which offer a variety of dim sims to create a kind of oriental smorgasbord meal. In American Chinese restaurants, you will find *dim sums* on the appetizer list.

Hot dogs in milk bars have many pseudonyms: **Saveloys** or **Savs** take their name from a popular brand. A **dagwood dog** denotes a frank skewered on a wooden stick, coated in batter and deep fried. You buy dagwoods at outdoor fetes (pronounced *fates* in Oz) from food stands or vending trucks. You will not find dagwood-style club sandwiches anywhere.

In a country that loves the ocean and all its bounty and was borne out of England, you would expect to find **fish and chips**. The street staple is as common in Oz as in Britain. Chips, of course, does not mean potato chips. Instead that refers to fat french fries. The fish can be any kind of **fillet** (that's FILET with the T pronounced). Often **flake** numbers among the choices. Flake is shark meat. Usually, you can choose to order fish either battered and deep fried or grilled on a commercial grill.

At the beach where takeaway fare beats carrying a heavy cooler, the gourmet fast food eater may find **prawn cutlets**, a batter-dipped butterflied shrimp. Make sure the frozen variety (most cheaper ones) get fully thawed before they deep fry them, otherwise you will donate your soggy lunch to the persistent flock of seagulls happily darting and soaring around you.

Sausages show up everywhere—at breakfast, lunch and supper, indoors and out. The most common barbecue phrase might be, "throw another **snag** on the **barby**." Snags mean sausages, just as **bangers** do. **Bangers** slip in from British-English in food phrases such as **bangers and mash**, or sausages and potatoes.

Alas, in recent history, American fast food has begun

to compete strongly with Aussie takeaway. Kentucky Fried Chicken encroached first, then McDonald's and Burger King arrived. The later under the *nom de plume* Happy Jack's. The primary dissimilarity between McDonald's U.S. and the Aussie counterpart is the advertising. While American commercials push all-American-kids style, the Aussie marketers promote "Australian-ness." One commercial jingle has sung the praises of pure Aussie beef and Tasmanian potatoes.

Thirsting for lemonade in the hot summer sun? Think again. It will be as hard to find as iced tea. **Lemonade** in Australia comes in a soda pop bottle. Ask for lemonade and you will always be served a carbonated lemon beverage similar to 7UP. The word **soda** by itself denotes soda water or club soda only, but you will never hear it called club soda. All flavored carbonated drinks fit in the **soft drink** category, much as in the States. Coke is Coke just about anywhere. If you don't want a carbonated soft drink, you may get a **cordial**. No, not the liqueur, but *cor-dee-ull*, a liquid version of Kool-Aid. Cordials are thick concentrated fruit flavorings bought by the bottle and mixed with water in your own kitchen. The trend is to mix cordials with naturally carbonated mineral water.

Once lunch passes and afternoon tea ends, it becomes time to think about supper. If visiting someone's home you may be invited to stay for **tea**—that means dinner, the whole dinner, not just a drink.

After this impromptu invitation, your host or hostess may apologize for serving **bubble and squeak,** or left-overs (though rarely would guests get anything out of **al-foil** for tea, except in a real pinch.)

One of the vegetables on the table may be pumpkin. "No," you say, "you make pies out of pumpkin, not a side dish." But in Oz, **pumpkin** describes the same veggie we call squash, as in **butternut pumpkin.** If you asked for **squash**, you'd get a beverage—a thick pulpy lemon or orange soda poured over crushed ice. So ask for squash instead of 7UP, and ask for **pumpkin** instead of squash; and, if you are in dire need of pumpkin pie wait for Thanksgiving in America!

A number of other vegetable names may throw you, too. Red beets are **beetroot**, and, as we said earlier, are commonly found sliced on sandwiches. **Silverbeet** is similar to Swiss chard. Broccoli can be pronounced *brock-col-EYE*. If a vegetable or any other food has been in the refrigerator for too long, you might notice it is **on the nose** or **gone off**, which means it has turned bad and stinks!

Like opposing camps in the kitchen, food breaks into two distinct tastes in Australia: **sweet** or **savoury. Sweet** can be anything candylike, fruity or creamy. **Savoury** lives in opposition. Anything not sweet includes paté, asparagus, cheese dips, cheeses, meats, whatever. The word **sweets** by itself generally means dessert and **savouries** swap places on the tray with canapés or hors d'oeuvres. Again, meaning depends on context.

Afters & Sweets

After dinner you'll be offered sweets with your coffee or tea. **Pavlova** numbers among the traditional favorites. **Pav** resembles a meringue-type dessert made of whipped egg whites and **heaps** (a substitute for lots of anything) of sugar. For children a real Aussie treat is a **lamington**. The **lam** resembles a square of chocolate sponge cake with shredded coconut all over it. The ever-loved **bickie** may show up on a plate once again. Any sweets may prove **moreish**, meaning you will want more of them!

One particular treat is an **Anzac biscuit**. It's the Australian version of an oatmeal cookie. Anzacs combine wheat flour, rolled oats, shredded coconut and golden syrup (the Aussie cane sugar syrup). History shows Anzacs were the popular homemade baked goods sent overseas to the troops, or **Anzacs**, during the First World War. Now kids take Anzacs to school for lunch. A.N.Z.A.C is an acronym for the Australian and New Zealand Army Corps who fought for the British Empire. More about them later.

If you have taken the kids to the movies and go for a snack afterwards, a very special treat to order will be a **spider**! Nothing bizarre or ghoulish here. Not a Halloween prank. Spiders claim kinship with ice cream sodas or floats. The recipe includes chocolate or other flavorings, soda water and ice cream.

Aussie kids are no different from kids the world over. They like their sweets. In particular, they like **lollies**—candy by another name. **Boiled lollies** refer to hard candy. Other names are different, too. **Fairy floss** dresses up a cotton candy stall and Aussies call chewing gum nothing more than **chewie**, never gum (maybe because that's what they call their most common trees!). The proper way to ask for gum is: **Can I bot a chewie**? This truly unique phrase raises the question: May I borrow (with no intention of returning) a piece of gum? In that sense, you can **bot** anything; and someone who **bots** all the time becomes known as a **bot**.

A person will always ask for a piece of chewie in Australia, never a stick of gum, as we do in America. The most common chewing gum brand, Wrigley's, does not sell sticks of chewie. Instead they sell candy-coated chiclet-type pellets packaged in wrappers very similar in size and design to those in which sticks are sold. If you are not careful opening the foil, you may have chewie everywhere! One flavor of chewie worth noting is Arrowmint—quite refreshing but a little different from American mint-flavored chewing gums.

Just as Hershey's markets itself as "The Great American Chocolate Bar," many brand names stroll hand in hand with Aussie childhood: **Violet Crumble** (crunchy honey and chocolate bar), **Jaffas** (jawbreakers), **Smarties** (like M&M's) **Cherry Ripe** (chocolate-covered cherry stuff) and **Minties** (chewy mint taffy squares). Everyone has his favorite **lolly**. Chocolate, by itself, falls victim to the clip-it-add-*y* syndrome — usually melted down to **chockie**. Hence, even an adult may find himself tempted by a **chockie bickie** or **chockie syrup** on ice cream.

Bugs & Crayfish

For truly fancy fare, Australians look to numerous seafood restaurants, numerous because all the major cities are port towns. The names of the delicacies might sound unfamiliar but the scrumptious foods are sought the world over, with one exception—**the bug.** Americans do not eat bugs! But these must be tasted because the name is a fallacy. The proper names for these little crustaceans is the **Balmain Bug** and **Moreton Bay Bug.** In truth, bugs are kin to lobsters—small versions, known as bay lobsters or shovel-nosed lobsters. The longer formal names tell a diner where the bug was caught. **Balmain** is a Sydney suburb on the coast of Sydney Harbour. Further north on the east coast, fishermen trap bugs in Moreton Bay off Brisbane, Queensland. Some gourmet palates claim the Balmain bug has a naturally garlicky flavor, distinct from that of its northern **rellie**. On a plate, bugs resemble small lobster tails split in half. A bug is mostly tail, with tiny abdominal sections and no claws to speak of.

By now, most Americans have heard the Paul Hogan phrase, "Throw another shrimp on the barby." Aussies are somewhat embarrassed by that because shrimp do not exist down under. All shrimp are called **prawns** no matter what size. All the way up to the huge **tiger** or **king prawns** the word shrimp never gets used. As the story goes, it was Hogan who changed the phrase from prawn to shrimp because he said Americans would never "catch it." Some Aussies say their prawns are so big that calling them shrimp would be an insult to the little crustacean. Also, **prawns on the barby** is a nouveau-sort of food, nothing the **oldies** would have thought about doing. They'll stick with the **bangers and snags, mate**.

The Down Under Bistro
MENU

ENTREES:
Barbecued Bugs
King Prawns
Oysters Kilpatrick
APPETISERS:
Pumpkin Soup
Tossed Salad
MAIN COURSE:
Rack of Spring Lamb
Veal Milanese
Honeyed Coral Trout
Crayfish
AFTERS:
Cheese and Greens
Creme Caramel
Pavlova with Kiwi Fruit

While food has different names on Aussie menus, the menus themselves look different. The use of the word entree regularly confuses Americans. Aussies use the term correctly. Entree has the connotation of "upon entering" or "first." So, the first choice on a menu Down Under is an **entree**. Appetisers (note the spelling) usually head the column of soups and salads. After them comes the **main course,** which is usually called the entree in America. Often, seafood or pasta can be ordered in either main-size or entree-size portions. Remember, the entree is smaller.

When sitting for a long leisurely dinner, you may not want to rush straight into dessert but rather wish to finish your wine with more savory tastes before choosing coffee and **sweets**. In that case, you may order **cheese and greens**. The combination platter plays the same role as cheese-and-crackers with some fresh fruit or veggies accompanying it.

Australians enjoy eating out (although it is not cheap). In Melbourne, **B.Y.O.** (or **B.Y.O.G.**) restaurants remain popular. That's where you can bring-your-own-grog, wine or beer usually. On a weekend, you may find it hard to get into a restaurant without reservations. **Book ahead** (rarely called "reserving"). The Aussies recommend it because popular eateries may be **chock-a-block** or **chocker** (sometimes **chockers**). That means chock-full, jammed or packed to the rafters.

Deli-restaurants have become fashionable in Australian cities, particularly ones with the moniker "gourmet" emblazoned across the window. They claim to be take-offs of New York delis, but they are a bit too **flash** or **swish** (fancy) for that. In Melbourne alone, three such restaurants with New York names have competed against one another: The New York Deli, Café Manhattan and The Wall Street Deli. Restaurants come and go quickly in any city and who knows how long the trend will last.

One delicatessen specialty not found Down Under is the corned-beef sandwich. The closest to corned beef you will find is **silverside**, a tough sinewy substitute. Anyway, you would be crazy to travel ten thousand miles to look for foods and other things that you can find in your backyard. Enjoy the differences, not the similarities.

Chapter 8

G'day, Mate

"Can I bot a chewie, **mate**?"
"Cheers, **mate**!"
"Whose **mate** is that?"
"Bring your **mates** along."
"That's Bobby's little **mate**."

All these sentences have one thing in common, the word **mate.** It's heard constantly throughout Australia. But what is a **mate?** A **mate** is the masculine synonym for friend, a buddy or pal. He could be a close co-worker, companion, teammate or neighbor. A father will call his son **mate,** a grandfather his grandson, an uncle his nephew. Mate is a catchy warm friendly phrase that men cannot help using. They've heard it all their lives and newcomers find it as comfortable as an old glove.

It's a compliment for one man to refer to another as a **mate of mine**. The fellow has been singled out as a good and true friend by this male endearment in its most fundamental form. **Best mates** is the highest plateau of comraderie or **mateship** among Australian males. Little boys have their best **mates** and adults do, too. "I'm going to the **footy** with my **mates** on Saturday," means the fellow is going with a close circle of friends, his best buddies.

While a mother may distinguish her son as **mate**

(perhaps readying the boy for the male world), most men do not like and do not expect to be referred to as **mate** by a woman. Mark that unacceptable! However, in recent years, more women co-workers characterize their male counterparts as **mates**, in general. But, hearing a woman say, "Thanks, mate," may bring a scowl to men's faces! It's just **not on** (not the way things are done)! She could get away with it in jest or sarcastically. Then, of course, everything is fair game.

Mate works as a generic label, as well, for the male stranger behind the store counter or for the man you've just been introduced to. It becomes a polite form of address, man to man. "How much for the sanger, **mate?"** Or when used in anger it sounds similar to a truck driver shouting: "Look, Mac, get off the road!" Substitute **mate** for Mac.

Digger can replace mate in conversation, though not frequently. The history of digger commands more interest. A digger was a miner who dug up the earth during the Australian gold rush of the 1850s. The digger's hard-working wife was a **diggeress.** Later, during World War One, the Aussie foot soldiers were renamed **diggers** during their service in the trenches fighting for Mother England. Once again Australians were carrying shovels but for an updated reason.

Those **khaki-clad** (pronounced *caa-key*) soldiers were the Anzacs, members of the Australian and New Zealand Army Corps. The Anzacs were the men in the **slouch hats** or **slouchies**. The hat has one side of the brim pinned or snapped up so it doesn't get in the way of the rifle carried over the soldier's shoulder. The **slouch** has become synonymous with Australia the world over.

Cobber can substitute for either **digger** or **mate,** but gets used even less frequently. Any man is a **bloke,** a fellow, a guy. But any bloke can be Fred or Norm—your average Joe. **Fred** or **Norm** star in most jokes, too. Even a nationwide public service fitness campaign starred a cartoon character named Norm. He was the epitome of the beer-swilling, overweight armchair athlete, and his presence has added Norm to the vocabulary, always meaning that hard-drinking, non-exercising bloke. When the answer to a question goes beyond obvious, the sarcastic response involves Fred: "Even **Blind Freddy** can see that!" Anyone could understand it, or know it, whatever it is!

On the same linguistic track, a woman is a **sheila.** While sheila does not flatter a woman, the name doesn't really degrade her either. It has a particular place in conversation, used only by men in reference to women. A woman would never characterize her friends as **sheilas.** Members of the female sex from teenagers on up may be referred to as **birds.** It's not too different from using chick to describe a woman, but it's spoken more often. Meantime, a little girl falls prey to rhyming slang in the phrase **Barossa pearl.** The rhyme stems from the Barossa Valley, the verdant wine-making region in the state of South Australia. As is their habit, the Aussies will clip the slang phrase and **barossa** alone becomes synonymous with girl.

Waltzing Matilda

Most Americans associate Australia with the song "Waltzing Matilda." The ballad tells the tale of the **swagman**, a central figure in Australian lore. The **swagman** is the paragon of the independent spirit of the Land Down Under, the stuff of which legends are made. A **swagman** or **swaggie** was marked by the bedroll or **swag** carried on his back, from which he takes his name. The **swaggie** was an itinerant who roamed the **outback** on foot in search of an occasional day's work in a town or on a **station** (ranch). He worked for bed and board. Sometimes his swag was a bluey because the blankets were made of blue wool. To **hump bluey** means to sling a bedroll across your back. The swag or bluey also went by a more affectionate name—**Matilda**—the lady he waltzed with throughout his dusty travels. To lead such a life was **to swag it**! A **sundowner** was the swaggie who arrived at sunset too late to do a day's work but hoped for tea and lodging anyway. Asking for a place to sleep was labeled **backslanging**. Another meaning of **sundowner** refers to men who worked a long day on the property and didn't return until sunset.

Cockies & Bushrangers

Like the swagman, farm life contributes to the strong spoken fabric Down Under. Generally, farmers accept the title **cockies**—once a derogatory term—now not so. It began with the beautiful white bird with the yellow crest, **the cockatoo**. While bird enthusiasts in America actively seek out cockatoos as exotic pets (remember the one in the *Baretta* television series?), in Australia they live in flocks flying above city rooftops or above the countryside at planting time. When a flock descends on a field, the cockatoos scratch around for seeds to eat. So farmers who tilled the often dry land were dubbed **cockatoos** or **cockies**.

From there, as words go in Oz, the definition's perimeter increased to encompass any **man-on-the-land**. A **cow-cocky** is a dairy farmer; a **sheep-cocky**, a sheep rancher; a **cane cocky**, a sugar cane plantation owner. The **boss cocky** is the landowner who has men working for him. **Weekend cockies** live in the city and own small plots of land as second homes. These uses led to the development of the obscure verb **to cockatoo**, meaning "to farm." One of the fancier terms used with a farmer's name is **pastoralist**, a man who runs sheep, and sometimes cattle or horses, in a large pastoral setting. But most such men on the land would rather be known as **graziers**. The owner of a small block of land gets reduced to a **blockie**. A **jackeroo** (or **jackaroo**) is not an animal as you might think. He is the apprentice on the station. Now, there's even a four-wheel-drive vehicle with the same name. The lady cowhand wears the title **jilleroo**.

The **bushie** or **bushman** spends his life in the outback or the **bush** (which is anywhere outside the cities). The **bushcook** serving Outback drovers on their long rides is the **snag**, just like all the sausages or **snags** he prepares. The rhyming substitution for cook is **babbling**

brook. Find more about farm life and bush words in Chapter Four.

Every country has its bandido. The **bushranger** belongs to Australia. Ned Kelly, in particular, looms as large in legend as Jesse James does. Kelly created a peculiar sensation in his last stand against police by wearing a suit of armor made of discarded tin. Any bad person is a **baddie,** the opposite of a "goody-goody." But, he may win the title **a bat lot** too—much like a bad penny.

While **baddie** can be easily understood, many other "people words" can be more difficult to understand, a favorite being **ocker** as in "He's just a bloody ocker!" You would describe this bloke as an unrefined Australian, a redneck or an embarrassing loud mouth. Norm, the cartoon character with a tinny in his hand, conjures up the ocker at his worst.

Right up there with the local ockers are the other loudmouthed rowdies: the **hoons** and the **larrikans**. Most often these insulting names befit young men who do foolish things for attention. They're blokes who rev car engines and squeal tyres outside the pub for the sake of being noticed. You know the type. In some parts of the country, however, a **hoon** specifically is a man who lives off prostitutes' money; but that's an obscure definition. It proves that usage and context form an important partnership in Aussie colloquial speech.

A **bludger** can fit this second less common meaning of **hoon** as well, according to the dictionary. But, generally a **bludger** will not pull his own weight. The bludger could be the fellow who watches his mates build a barbecue without ever laying a brick and expects to eat from it later. They'll complain, "That bludger will use this barby over my dead body!" Or they might say, at their most colorful, "That bludger wouldn't work in an iron lung" (Where he would't even have to breathe!). Someone singled out for being **on the dole** (the govern-

G'day, Mate

©1993 J. Colquhoun

ment welfare roles) for no good reason becomes a **dole-bludger.**

A **bodgie** once was considered a worthless person, but in the 1950s the name transferred to a group of "greasers" who proudly wore the emblem. Monosyllabic words seem to reign in this section and that suits the Aussies. A **bab** babbles on and on. A **poon** lives like a hermit in a remote area, often considered a fool because he is naive or unworldly to the point of hurting himself. **Berk** or **nark** labels a thoroughly unpleasant person, someone to stay as far away from as possible.

Much sweat has been expelled coining words that berate people as stupid or lazy, so the nomenclature continues in its whimsical manner. Because **dilly** rhymes with silly it has the identical meaning. Somehow from that beginning the Australians adopted **dills** or **dillpots** as substitutions for dummy. **Blinky Bill** rhymes with dill and conveys the same idea, too. The real Blinky Bill is an Australian storybook character, a mischievous koala who always **gets into strife** (another expression Aussies use more than Americans. Under **dill** include **bunny** (as in dumb bunny) and **drongo**. A slow-witted race horse named **Drongo** in the 1920s had a penchant for coming in last. Now, **drongo** defines anyone considered slow to catch on, in tribute to that dumb horse.

Pimp in Australia is not what you're thinking. A pimp is a tattletale. When you're tattling on someone you're **pimping** on them, as children do. In that sense, it wouldn't be unheard of for a child to cry, "Mummy, Joey's a pimp!"—startling to an American. Because of their height or lack of it, a small child unaffectionately gets tagged an **anklebiter** and preschool and primary grades are **anklebiter schools**. **Littlies** may be called **bub** or **bubby** with more affection. "The little bub" may refer to a boy or girl. You see, the cutting tongue spares no one in any sector of society.

More Occupations

If you get into strife with the law you'll need a **solicitor** to help you out, but if you go to court you'll be represented by a **barrister**. Australia, as other Commonwealth countries once under English rule, follows the British judicial system right down to the wearing of wigs, ruffles and gowns in the court. The barrister's clerk (*clark*) or secretary, or anyone's secretary for that matter, wears the moniker **shiny bottom** because he wears out his pants from sitting all day long.

To fill a prescription you'll need a **chemist,** not a pharmacist—so do not look for a pharmacy on the corner. You'll find the **chemist** instead. A surgeon is called **mister,** not doctor; and nurses are **sisters**. A **compere** hosts a television show or a stage event, just as an emcee does in the U.S. Emcee, of course, is an American bastardized construction, extracted from the initials M.C., the acronym for master of ceremonies. The TV news anchorman or anchorwoman is the **news presenter** of the **bulletin**—which is what Australians call the newscast.

No Antipodean colloquial list in any category would be complete without a group of clipped words. An airline stewardess has been retitled **hostess** which is always trimmed to **hostie.** Here are some others: **brickie,** a bricklayer; **deckie,** a deckhand on a boat; **flaggie**, a flagman at a road construction site. A **derro** is a derelict on the street (not unlike wino) and a **reffo** is a refugee. Again these terms on first hearing may not sound flattering, but they are not meant to be degrading either. Write it off to being a part of the relaxed Australian way of life, nothing more, nothing less.

The Aussie Battler

Another whole class of people in Australia are the **Aussie battlers.** They are not a club or an organization. The term befits the everyday Australian. An **Aussie battler** is the average working person who's always trying to get ahead, to get more out of life, to get more from his salary, but never quite gets out from behind the eight ball. He keeps battling anyway. The battler means a great deal to Australians—probably from their colonial roots—men fighting a system that was harder, tougher and crueler than they were; men fighting nature which was strong and fierce. Today the Aussie battler is the working man, who has a bit less than what he wants. In colloquial speech, the battler labels people with all sorts of strife. A person fighting a physical handicap is a battler; the widow left with several children is a battler; the old man trying to get through the day is a battler. People who hang the moniker on someone else say it with pride in their commitment, courage and persistence. "A real **battler,** that one!" they will say as they take their hats off to him.

Chapter 9

Aussie Subcultures

In Australia, a few entities have created large chunks of language and donated them to the mainstream. They deserve a separate mention.

As written in the travel section, bush culture and station life have enriched the language with terms for clothing and animals and everyday phrases which have changed meaning with time, but because they are inherently Australian, Aussies will always find a use for them.

The great Aussie pub constitutes a subculture and has a language unique to that setting.

Aborigines have given greatly to Aussie-English. Their words not only describe the flora and fauna of the island nation and their unique events and places but some aboriginal words and sounds have wound their way into modern kitchens and newspapers as well.

Station Life & the Bush Telegraph

Along the way, we've met the **swaggies**, the **cockies**, the **jilleroos** and **jackeroos**—the real-life characters from Australia's **bush** (country) but we haven't been introduced to some of the phrases turned by Aussie station dwellers. Remember it's here where the **cocky, the grazier** and the **pastoralist** remain king (more later). Now meet the **squatter,** another landowner! (Obviously not so in inner city New York or London.) It stems from the early years of Australia. The closest thing to a squatter in America was a homesteader.

Picture the Australia of Colleen McCullough's **The Thornbirds**, a vast cattle **station** (ranch) which never seems to end. The **home paddock** surrounds the main house. A **paddock** in Oz does not connote only a turf field for grazing. Instead, any field is a paddock, whether corn shoots up from the ground as straight as toy soldiers or whether cows graze lazily on golden hay. The **back paddock** compares to the "North 40," the section of the property farthest away from the house.

Barns do not stand in the farmyards of most of Australia (with the exception of a few areas settled by Germans, notably the Barossa Valley). Most farm buildings fall under the heading **shed.** Every outbuilding, expansive or tiny, is a **shed.** Station owners construct most sheds out of corrugated tin and aluminum—the walls as well as the roof. Many have only three sides. The **chooks** live in a shed, albeit a little one. A **chook**? A **chook** is a chicken, a hen old enough to lay eggs or be roasted for Sunday dinner. A little **chook** is actually called a **chicken.** Don't worry, they've left the rooster alone.

On the cattle station, young bull calves sold for veal can be called **mickey calves** or **bobby calves**. A **mickey** is usually the wildest calf in the bunch. The **poddy calf** may live among the mickeys and the bobbies, too. It is the orphan which must be fed by hand. You raise a **poddy lamb** the same way.

Most farms have man-made ponds somewhere on the grounds, sometimes for the animals, sometimes for irrigation. Australian farms have them, too, but they do not call them ponds or waterholes. They are **dams**. It's strange to hear that cows drink from dams and children swim in dams, but Down Under they do. In the hot summer, kids may also dive into a **bogie**, another word for swimming hole. With nothing better to do, the youngsters may lie back and count all the clouds in the **apple pie**! What? Remember the rules for rhyming slang. Pie rhymes with sky. That solves it.

Driveway is too fancy a word as far as Aussie cockies are concerned. They prefer to call their driveways **tracks**. Tracks can be any unpaved road surface throughout a property, like the track to the shearing shed or the back paddock. Paved surfaces are referred to as **bitumen**. That's *bitch-u-men*, their version of blacktop or asphalt.

On a sheep station, the shearers in the **shearing shed** or **wool shed** have a language all their own. Here are a few examples: The **broomie** sweeps up the floor and separates the **dags** from the wool. Dags are the sheep "dirt" (a familiar euphemism, I trust) and other "crud" caught in the fleece around the animals' bottom. These unpleasantries are mentioned because the word dag has been carried off the station and gladly transported to the cities. A dag now denotes an outcast, someone unsociable or untrendy, who "dresses **daggy**" or "wears **daggy** clothes." He may be classified as "such a **dag**!"—a stigma shunned by all.

A young shearer aspires to be the **ringer**, the top shearer in the shed—it's most likely the source of our colloquial sports term "ringer." The **board-boy** stands alongside the **broomie** as another wool shedhand. When the shearers and the boys are ready for a break, they take a **smoko**. A smoko originally meant stopping for a smoke, but then the definition widened to mean a break—a cigarette and/or a cup of tea or coffee and a snack, any kind of break from hard **yakker**. Even a brochure for a riding school advertises "Full afternoon bush rides (smoko included) for experienced riders only." The **smoko** in that case means they stop and supply tea and a biscuit midway through the ride.

Aussie slang for a cigarette has been stolen from the British. Instead of a "butt," someone will ask for a **fag**. Remember, fag does not carry the American slang connotation. On a weekend, the shearers, broomies and folks from the surrounding district may get invitations to a **woolshed hop**, just an old-fashioned barn dance or hoedown.

One of the trained sheep dogs is the **backing dog**. He brings up the rear of the flock or **the mob**. While mob means flock in this case, any group of people or things in Oz gets dubbed a mob. Perhaps the worst parts of station life are the **blowies** and the mozzies. They create tandem trouble. Blowies, short for blowflies, are flies, and **mozzies** are mosquitoes. Whatever they're called, they still buzz and sting the same. There just seem to be more of them in Australia. Together the blowies and the mozzies gave birth to an important piece of Australiana—**the Aussie salute**. **Salute** befits the act of swatting flies away from the face, a constant activity in the bush. Hardcore **swagmen** and **bushies** wore corks dangling from their hat brims to keep the blowies away.

The **cockies** come to town for **The Royal Show**, and if your travel schedule finds you in town for The Show, go! It can be quite a treat. **The Show** compares with American state fairs. Primarily an agricultural show, city families flock to it as well to see the prize bulls, the baking contests, crafts displays, lumberjacks and you name it. Each region has an annual show where kids scurry to get their **showbags**. They began as sample giveaways, full of surprises, but now they're filled with everything from snack food to Barbie® doll supplies, sold virtually for the price of their contents.

More bush words tumble into the language of the house just as they do into most sectors of the Australian lexicon. To see the countryside, you take a **bushwalk**. **Bushwalking** ranks as a rather modern term which basically means leisure hiking, day-hiking or nature walking. Travelers will hear it offen as a description of things to do in parkland or nature preserves.

An old-fashioned household cure—something grandmother might hand down—is a **bush-cure**. A bush-cure comes in handy when someone feels **crook**, which means they're sick (possibly taken from the German *krank*). Maybe they ingested some bad **bush tucker**—simple campsite fare. The neighborhood grapevine has nothing over the **bush telegraph** when it comes to spreading gossip, rumor or even useful information.

the Outback
Akubra
Driz-a-Bone
Moleskins
R.M. Williams boots

Country Clothes/City Fashions

On the farm or station, a few other "musts" exist. **Gumbies** block the back doorway of the house when not covering feet to save them from mud or dung. Gumbies or **gumboots** describe any kind of rubber boots, also known as **Wellingtons** or **Wellies**—the last two terms handed down by the British.

The signs of a grazier are his **Driz-a-Bone** and **Akubra**. The Driz-a-Bone trademark is derived from the phrase "dry as a bone" and befits the heavy brown oiled-cotton overcoat worn by stockmen and farmers. The cotton breathes in the heat and cold, and the oil creates the same effect as oil in a duck's feathers. Water rolls right off. The Akubra brand name tags many stockmen's hats throughout bush country. At first glance the hats resemble American cowboy hats but a keen eye can spot variations in styles between the American West and the Australian bush. Other hatmakers create bush headgear but Akubra is certainly the best known.

Another classic is the **R.M. Williams** boot. It is ankle high and has a narrow top with thick elastic insets to give it a tight fit on the leg. The tightness at the ankle deters the creepy-crawlies from slithering out of the bush and sneaking inside shoes. To keep creatures from going the other direction, up the pants leg, tie **bowyangs** around the fabric. Bowyangs are usually leather shoestrings, but any string or fabric can do the job.

Moleskins share the same closet with the rest of the bushgear. These traditional buff-colored pants follow the style of Western jeans, but, instead of denim, they are made of a soft brushed cotton fabric called moleskin. Like Western clothing in the U.S., bush clothes had a revival in Australia, making boots, hats and moleskins trendy for city wear as well as country gear, and sending prices skyrocketing.

Inside the Pub

Drinking garners a great deal of time in this land of long hot summers. (Stiff **drink driving** laws are changing the scene somewhat but Australia wouldn't be Australia without its pubs!)

Pub and **hotel** are interchangeable words in most cases, dating back to the old laws (many of which exist today). The enforced laws commanded any establishment selling liquor to provide food and accommodations. So even packaged beer, wine and hard liquor is sold at the pub annex, called the **bottle shop**. Parts of America have bottle shops, too, but nowhere but Australia has **drive-in bottle shops**, where you drive under an archway and a **bloke** serves you at your car. He then happily pops a case or two of **tinnies** in the **boot** or gives you the run down on cold wines. If you need time to browse the shelves, you pull over, get out and let the next car through. It's very organized.

You can find a pub anywhere—city, country, back streets or main road. In rhyming slang, the pub is a **rub-a-dub**, **a rubbity-dub** or just a **rubbity** (also spelled **rubbidy**). Pubs have been male domain always. That is not to say women cannot drink in a pub, but it is still a male-oriented place—at least in the section called the **public bar**. That's where the men stand around and **hit the turps** (any alcohol, shortened form of turpentine).

Rhyming slang gets spread thickly where liquor loosens the tongue. Men swill **pig's ear** (beer) or **mother's sin** (gin). Another bloke may order **aunty's downfall** (also gin) or a glass of **plonk** or **bombo**. The latter rank low on the wine list.

Ordering beer is an art. You might order a **pony**, **middy** or **schooner**. This list has nothing to do with the kind of beer you drink just the size of the glass in which it is served. The names differ among the states. A **schooner** is a big 15-ounce glass. (Ounce is a throwback to before Australia went metric.) A **middy** equals ten ounces in New South Wales and a **pot** means the smaller glass in other states. A regular glass gets called creatively **a glass**, filled with seven ounces of beer. The tiniest glass, not often found, is the five-ounce **pony**.

To bounce from pub to pub in a given night is to do the **pub crawl**, the Aussie version of bar-hopping. And if you intend to party hearty all night long, you and your friends are out for a **rage** or **gone raging**. The expression the next morning might be, "I've got a hangover. We **raged** all night!"

The guy who buys the round announces: "It's my **shout**," or in rhyming slang, he might insist on his **wally grout**. The phrase gets stretched in other ways. If friends intend to treat someone in their circle for a birthday or other occasion, they will **shout** them a meal.

You can, of course, have lunch in a pub. Usually you order from a blackboard menu, pay at the counter and get served by a waitress. According to tradition, pubs serve lunch strictly between noon and two p.m. Not a moment later. They serve dinner between six and eight. In some areas, this custom is changing, but, if you are in the countryside and aren't sure, don't risk missing pub hours. You may find yourselves at the **milk bar** for a meal.

Gifts from the Aborigines

The word Aborigine itself is, of course, not native to Australia. It stems from *ab origine*, Latin for "from the origin." The Aborigines are like Native Americans, a collection of tribes and families who white men lumped together under one banner.

Aboriginal culture, its myths and legends have enriched Australian language. Not only are aboriginal place names filled with history but so are many of the colloquialisms which slide off the Aussie tongue so easily. Without aboriginal languages there would be no kangaroo or koala. They may have been given Anglo names instead.

The cry "**coo-ee**!" was once used to catch another's attention while walking through the bush where you could not be seen but might be heard. "Coo-ee" originates with the aboriginals who probably mimicked a bush bird's call. Since then, modern phrases have developed, such as:

"I can't believe I missed you at the mall Saturday. You must have been **within coo-ee**." (within the sound of my voice).

At a track meet, a disappointed coach might say: "My team wasn't **within coo-ee** of the finish."

Also, "Coo-ee!" can be an exclamation, substituting for "Wow!"

Billy represents much more than a boy's name in Oz. Mainly, **billy** equals a makeshift pot or tin can in which water is boiled over a campfire, usually for tea (a camp pot). A swaggie always carries a billy or a **billycan**. The billycan may have started out as an old coffee tin. **Billy tongs** pick the hot pot off the campfire and pour the **billytea**. In these usages, billy derives its name from the Aborigine word **billa**, meaning water.

An overflowing river or creek creates a **billabong** or a

small runoff pond along its bank, a perfect calm spot to set up camp.

Walkabout means what it sounds like—to go walking about or **go for a wander**. But **walkabout** is connected directly with the Aborigines. Something in their heritage draws them back to their traditional homeland from time to time during their lives. The call may come at any time, no matter what other commitments the person might have. It's believed they return to their ancestral land for a kind of spiritual replenishment. While the serious meaning of walkabout stands, the word has other connotations now. Anyone can go walkabout, whether to take a break for a few hours or take time off from work for a few days. Or it can just mean going walkabout after dinner on a lovely evening.

A **willy-willy** is a wind funnel filled with dust or sand which dances across a dry paddock, a dusty street or along a beach.

Other aboriginal-based words slither softly through the language of the Antipodes. A **corroboree** is a celebration, a festival. The music of an aboriginal corroboree comes from the **didgeridoo** (pronounced *did-jer-ree-DO*), a primitive woodwind instrument that releases an eerie sort of melody. A **dillybag** serves as a small carrier sack and a **humpy** describes a crude mud brick dwelling.

Chapter 10

Dinky-di Australian

Early white settlers in Australia were a combination of free men and women and convicts known as **transportees**, those transported by ship from Britain to serve a prison sentence in the penal colony, starting in 1788 after the American Revolution. Together they were the equivalents of America's pioneers. Caught in the twin grips of being tenants in an unknown world and living as an underclass, they became master wordsmiths. The new vocabulary combined Anglicized aboriginal words, the melding of Scotch, Irish, Welsh, Cockney and other English dialects with new words born out of necessity.

The Never-Never

Aussies have a long list of names for remote locations not understood by most Americans, and they sound just as silly as "the boonies." The **boo-ay** or **up the boo-ay** (pronounced *boo-EH*) describes any outlying district. Today **the Never-Never** puts you in a similar spot. When you **wander the Never-Never**, you're on **the wallaby track** or off to **woop woop**, in each case heading "God-knows-where." You can ask for credit on **the never-never plan** and pay it off forever, with interest, of course. In modern terms, any use of a credit card might be called **the never-never plan**. The phrase is a holdover from the British, though it sounds more Australian these days.

Back of beyond and **back of Bourke** list as two more synonyms for somewhere in the **Outback**. Bourke is the last New South Wales town on the edge of the great desert that fills the center of the Australian continent. A horserider would say of his mate, "He's been gone for a long time, probably **back of beyond** by now." Meanwhile, he could have ridden **beyond the black stump**, a legendary spot, and wind up in the same place that going **back of Bourke** took him, anywhere in the outback. Some towns in Australia claim to be home of the original **black stump** of legend—the charred remnants of a tree—but no town father has ever proved the phrase pointed to a real and not imaginary place. Once a person is lost, he may find himself in the **backblocks**, away from the main street or on the outskirts of town. Backblocks translates into back streets also.

Lots of Blue

Blue fills a lot of gaps in the Aussie nomenclature. They nickname redheaded boys **Blue** or **Bluey**, instead of naming them "Red," a play on words at a redhead's expense. Remember, we said **bluey** is the swagman's blue wool bedroll, too. To **make a blue** means to make a mistake; and the guy who **cops the blue** takes the blame for it. Too much turps leaves a man **blue** (drunk) and that could bring on a **blue** in the pub (a fight or a brawl).

In addition to a blue, a **punch-up** may be a **stoush**, a **box-on**, a **barney** or a **boil-up**. A boil-up takes place when anger boils over. The barney could be brought on by an argument or an **argy-bargy** (argumentative) bloke. He's the kind of guy that gets **toey** (jumpy) in a crowd. At this point, the pub owner turns **ropeable** (fit to be tied) and his **cheese and kisses** (Mrs.) grows **aggro** (aggravated) with the lot of them. You can also have a

blue at home, which would be an argument rather than a punch-up.

Fair Dinkum

Fair dinkum once meant, literally, "honest work." Now, it stands for "honestly." The phrase is truly Australian. The genuine article gets labeled **dinkum Aussie**. It has even worked its way into government tourism campaigns. The Aussies embrace "dinkum" from the time they are children and do not let go. A mother may ask her child if he's telling the truth and the boy could reply, "**Fair dinks**, Mum." Or "Honest, Mom." The most commonplace use of fair dinkum is when someone tells a tall story, and the listener asks in disbelief: "Fair dinkum?" The reply might be, "Dinkum, Mate" or even better, "She's dinky-di." True Blue.

Yakker comes dressed in brown overalls or navy blue laborers' shorts, covered with sweat. "Building that fence in the hot sun was **hard yakker**!" Or a farmer who bought a plot of bad land has a hard yakker ahead of him. Yakker can mean nothing less than heavy work.

Taking the Mickey Out

When an event heats up in America, it **hots up** Down Under. Heating up and **hotting up** are twins. When something exciting or out of the ordinary happens, out come the **sticky beaks** hand-in-hand with the "nosey bodies." Sticky beaks stick their noses or beaks into other people's business. A sticky beak can **take a sticky beak** too, by "nosing around" or browsing. Sometimes the whole phrase will be shortened to **having a sticky** or **taking a sticky**. If you go to visit a friend's new home for the first time, you may ask to **have a sticky,** a look around. But a **sticky beak** may also be a snoop—putting a nose in where it's not supposed to be.

When you relate embarrassing or off-color stories you

split a bibful. The receiver winds up with **a bibful** when you're done telling tales. The bibful of gossip may be out-and-out lies. On the other hand, it could be **spot on** or **bang on** the truth; in which case, the teller "hit the nail on the head." But if it's all in fun and everyone is just teasing, they are **taking the mickey out of you!** Aussies absolutely love to **take the mickey out** of someone at any given time, especially a **Yank** new to the place and the language.

Happy as Larry

"Your new car is just **beaut**! You must be **happy as Larry, mate!**" It's terrific, wonderful, great! Beaut can describe anything but it is always a compliment, unlike "beaut" in American slang which more than likely is sarcastic and negative. In the U.S. you might call a rude person "a beaut."

Bonzer! and **grouse**! double as beaut's best Aussie mates. Grouse has been adopted as an Aussie teen-age term, something a Down Under "Val-gal" might say. If something is beyond terrific, beyond wonderful, call it **ripper**! A great buy is a **ripper**. A fan at a **footy** match may shout "**ripper!**" at the end of a big play. In search of another compliment to serve, try "**good on ya!**"—a way of saying "You've done well. We're proud of you."

The bloke **tinny** (lucky) enough to win an Aussie lotto will be **rapt** when the money arrives in a lump sum. Rapt comes from "in rapture." Someone else will be **happy as Larry** when life goes his way. Some oral tradition says the **Larry** in the phrase stems from the word **larrikan** which originally meant a fool. But **Larry** has moved away from that definition and now he's the happiest man in the world.

The same bloke will tell you, "No worries!" "Everything's **apples**!" or "She's **apples**!" Just as likely, he'll exclaim, "**She**'s sweet!" "She," in this context, replaces "everything" as in the idiom "**She'll be right, mate**." The translation is "Things will get better," or to use another Aussie expression, "It'll **come good.**" To **come good** can move in similar circles in relation to people. If a guy owes you money but you believe he'll repay you, you would comment, "He'll come good." Similarly, a kid who has been notoriously bad all along might "come good in the end" by changing his ways and going straight.

Rafferty's Rules

Another myriad of phrases describes times "when things go bad." A deal turns sour and the bloke making the deal **comes a cropper**. "Fred's business was doing so well, then it **came a cropper** (hit the skids)." Fred may try for a desperate comeback by betting on **Sydney or the bush**, which means he's going for all or nothing and he may wind up with a **basinful of trouble**. With a basinful like that, Fred does not have "a chance in Hell" of turning things around and that measures up to having **Buckley's chance**. Poor **Buckley** had no chance at all. The etymology of "Buckley's chance" has blurred badly with time. Some say it stems from William Buckley, an early escaped convict who lived among Aborigines with no chance of ever returning to Great Britain. (By the way, this William Buckley would have been an *es-ca-PEE*, not an *es-CAPE-ee*.)

An independent man might live by **Rafferty's rules**, meaning no rules at all—another blurry etymology here. Like **Buckley, Rafferty** may have begun as a slight aimed at Irish immigrants or convicts, since both are Irish surnames adopted as colloquial speech. No matter how the phrases began, it is clear now that when you live by **Rafferty's rules,** you will have **Buckley's chance** of escaping the law!

When a person is confused and doesn't know whether he's coming or going, the Aussies say he doesn't know **if he's Arthur or Martha**! But, if he knows exactly where he's heading and he is seeking adventure, he's probably

as game as Ned Kelly. That's ready and willing to undertake anything put before him, just like the **bushranger** Ned Kelly did in his legendary lifetime. Over the years, Kelly and his gang covered more than a few miles on the **frog and toad** (rhyming slang for road) running from the police.

To Whinge Is to Whine

Whining and complaining equal **whinging** and the whiner gets labeled a **whinger**. Mum scolds the whining child, "Don't **whinge**!" And a co-worker fed up with someone's constant complaining will refer to the person as a **real whinger**. A person who has nothing to whinge about and has become outstanding in his or her field falls into the **tall poppy** category. A **tall poppy** is an achiever who becomes well known in the process—a notable. Most tall poppies gain their status through positive means in government positions or industry. Others might be entertainers or communicators, doctors or research scientists. Most people work very hard to become tall poppies, some possibly to the point of exhaustion. At the end of each day, they're **all in** or **buggered**. When they're that tired, they may **bugger up** by making a mistake (or a **blue**). But to try and fail beats **doing bugger all**—which means doing nothing whatsoever. The **bludger** whom we've met before goes through life doing **bugger all**!

Stuffed!

After a sumptuous meal where you've consumed everything in sight you may feel stuffed. Fair enough! But, if an Aussie tells you, "**Get stuffed**!" he's not talking about eating. **Stuffed**, here, has the same foul connotation as the four-letter word which you could imagine in its place. Not polite at all.

If you do slip up, "**No worries**!" (Don't worry). The

Aussies will just **take the mickey** out of you for a little while.

Hello and Good-bye

Everyone knows Aussies say, "**G'day**." That's the contraction for "Good Day" but they not only contract the spelling but the sound as well. The *good* is just a quick *g* sound rolled off the tongue and squashed against the *day*. It has become their universal greeting, unique among English-speaking people.

For good-bye, you will hear other phrases which sound a bit British. "**Cheers**!" is one. Of course, "Cheers!" may also be a toast with a drink in hand. But, if someone says it walking out the door, you know they mean, "So long, farewell." In addition to cheers, **hooroo** shows up, as another old-fashioned salutation you hear instead of "see you later."

Chapter 11

Getting Through the Day

Jumpers and Windcheaters

On a cool afternoon Down Under you have a choice of **jumpers**, **cardies**, **sloppy joes** or **windcheaters** to fight the chill. An interesting set of choices! The first two are sweaters and the second pair substitutes for sweat-shirts. But what job in the wardrobe do each of these perform? You may be surprised.

Women wear **jumpers** and so do men! There's nothing strange about a man or a boy in a **jumper** because jumper fills the same place in the drawer as a pullover of any kind. It could be a **rugby** or **footy jumper**. Then again, it may be a fine hand-knitted jumper made of the best **merino** wool or a workman's jumper created from **greasy wool**. Greasy doesn't mean dirty. It's the Aussie term for the kind of wool with natural lanolin present, used in many countries particularly for sailing sweaters and hats. The natural oil keeps water from seeping into the knit. Obviously, this **jumper** would never get con-fused with the woman's sleeveless dress worn over a blouse. Women do wear similar frocks in Oz but they call them **pinafores** or **pinnies**.

Polo jumpers refer to turtleneck sweaters, with **polo collar** standing in for turtleneck. Polos never mean the summery knit shirts Americans wear. They're just collared sport shirts. The Aussie word-clippers use **cardie** as an excuse for cardigan. No real mystery there! But it is quite cute to hear an elderly couple remind each other to bring a **cardie** along. While sloppy joes in the U.S.A. are those saucy ground meat sandwiches, the Aussies have chosen to call sweatshirts that instead. I suppose someone in a fleecy **jumper** was told once he looked like a "Sloppy Joe" and the name stuck! A **windcheater** makes more sense. You put a pullover on "to cheat the wind"—but Americans might choose a windbreaker over a sweatshirt for the same purpose.

On a very cold day, Australians will be happy to put on a **skivvy** to go outside! Crazy? Not really. A skivvy is a cotton long-sleeved turtleneck, not underclothes. You may think you know what **knickers** are when people talk about them. But, be careful! Knickers are ladies' underpants. It probably stems from a time when undergarments were knee length, like bloomers. Today, knickers mean even the tiniest, laciest briefs.

In different regions, swimwear varies by name. It could be **bathers**, **togs** or **cozzies**. The odd one in the bunch, cozzie, takes its name from the clipped version of **bathing costume.** Get it? Along with togs, Aussies slip on a pair of **thongs**, the cheap rubber sandals called by several names in the U.S. **Sandshoes** are mandatory for reef walking so you do not cut your feet. They are not special gear, just sneakers.

Men who work outdoors have an unofficial uniform for workday dress. It consists of navy blue short shorts known as **stubbies**, after a brand name, and navy blue **singlets** made of cotton or wool.

School Days

Australian children either attend **state schools** or **public schools**. That sounds like the same thing, but it is not. **State schools** equal our public schools; state-run, meaning publicly-funded schools. **Public schools** are just the opposite of what they sound like. They are the private schools, equivalent to the British preparatory schools. The first year in school is **kindie**, a truncated form of kindergarten. (Kindergarten, you may want to note, is adopted from the German. The direct translation is "children's garden.") A **college** is very often a high school or secondary school but it can be attached to the name of any private school. It is not the equivalent of university. Therefore, if an Australian begins a story, "When I was at college . . . ," he is probably talking about his teen years. The students at a university answer to the name **uni students**, never co-eds.

Children wear uniforms to both state and public schools. They are similar to the uniforms worn in American parochial schools. Little girls don **pinnies**; older girls, wool skirts and blazers in winter; and both age groups have lightweight dresses for the summer months. Boys usually wear gray flannel trousers and blazers. But uniform shorts enter the summer-time picture, especially for the **littlies** (make that "little ones"). Shorts and summer frocks are important in Oz because the days can get very hot.

The kids do not get three months summer vacation. Instead, they get a six-week **holiday** (vacation) during the Christmas period (which remember is the height of summer) and a couple of weeks here and there during the rest of the calendar year. Each school year begins in January, after the Christmas break.

Older girls may bring **handbags** to school but no girl or woman in Australia ever carries a "pocketbook." According to them, a pocketbook is strictly American. Children living in Queensland tote their school books to and from school in a **port**. That is the shortened version of portmanteau, a word used by the British to mean suitcase, obviously borrowed from the French. **Port** generally means any small carrying case or bookbag in Queensland, but nowhere else in the country.

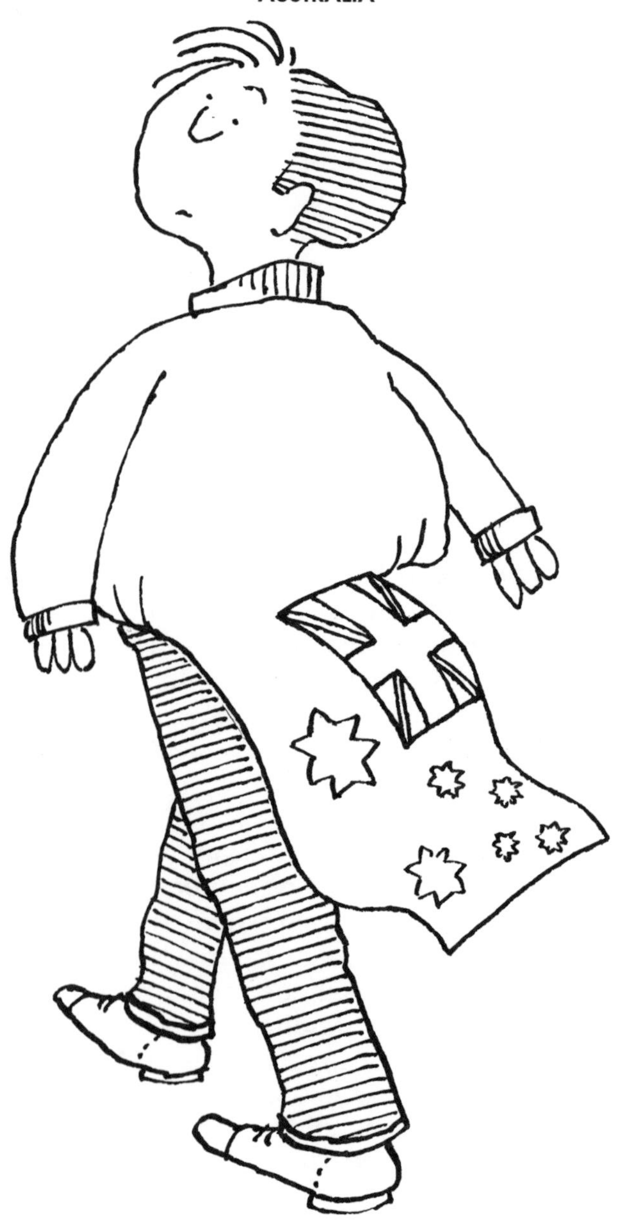

the Australian flag

In addition to most of the paraphernalia kids carry to and from school, Aussie kids take **rubbers** along too. No, it's not rainy. They don't bring galoshes with them everywhere, just **rubbers**. Rubbers are rubber pencil erasers, nothing else. Hats comprise an important part of the school uniform. Wool felt **tit-fors** (remember tit-for-tat rhymes with hat) partner with winter clothes; old-fashioned straw boaters and girls' bonnets with long ribbons down the back are part of the summer dress code.

Little girls may have **fringe** under their hats and long **plats** (or **plaits**) down the sides. **Plats** and **fringe** have nothing to do with the hats; they are a part of the girl's hairstyle. Fringe substitutes for bangs and plats are braids. Instead of braiding hair, Mum **plats** her daughter's hair. An unkempt little digger may add an **Australian flag** to his uniform. Some say it's the official dresswear of Oz. It means the little guy's shirttail is hanging out the back of his pants and waving about like a flag! Mum or dad may give children an allowance to pay for school items, and they might say, "Put it in your **kick**." The kick fills the same gap as "kitty," a place to put your money.

Around the House

The rooms, furniture and parts of an Australian house have many labels which differ from those used in America. Even the living room has not been spared. Families sit in their **lounge rooms**, as if they were a public waiting room. They purchase **lounge suites** (matching sofa, chairs, etc.) to fill the lounge.

While visiting a private home, you may need to avail yourself of a toilet. Things are changing, but this simple undertaking may be a bit more complex than you would imagine. The **toilet** is just that, a little room with a toilet in it, sometimes accompanied by a sink, but not necessarily! Sometimes Australians refer to the **loo**, which is a carryover from the British. If you really want to freshen up, inquire about the bathroom. But, keep in mind, the bathroom may not have a toilet in it! The fine line drawn between **toilet** and **bathroom** and the existence of sinkless toilets and toilet-less bathrooms stems from the late 50s and early 60s when the **dunny** finally gave way to sewage. The dunny sits comfortably alongside the outhouse in history but outlived the American ones by decades. In modern homes, a full bath adjoining a bedroom takes on the fancy French phrase *en suite*. **En suite** in Australia has come to mean only the bedroom/bathroom arrangement. Nothing else.

In the kitchen, a number of differences catch the cook's eye. Cookbooks must be translated like foreign novels for the American recipe reader. To begin with, Australia follows the metric system, which means a cup measures more than a U.S. cup, though it sounds the same. All measures need to be converted. Recipes call for **corn flour** instead of corn starch. You won't find baking soda either, only bicarbonate of soda. Both red or green peppers are **capsicums**. Like veggies in the U.S., vegetables have taken on pet names: **mushies**, **'nanas** and **avos** (mushrooms, bananas and avocados) to name a few.

Broiled meat and fish cook in a **griller** and come out **grilled**. The **electric jug** or **electric kettle** replaced the **billy** indoors in Australia. The electric pot may be a **birko** also, a tradename now in common use around the house. All of them make a quick **cuppa** (cup of tea or coffee) and that's important! You set the table with **serviettes**, another word from the French, not napkins. **Napkins** have another job and it has to do with baby. Look for napkins or **nappies** where you would find diapers, maybe next to the **cot**. While cot always denotes a crib, it may refer to any size bed, depending on the context. **Jumping in the cot** means jumping in the sack or hitting the hay. A man may be surprised to learn he can **nurse** a baby Down Under. Anyone cuddling or holding a little one **nurses** the child. In this way, nursing is not synonymous with breast-feeding.

When Australians need bed sheets and towels for their homes they shop for **manchester**. The **manchester department** carries all household linens. The name reflects history. Manchester, England, was a textile town. Bedding shoppers do not bother looking for "January white sales" because linens do not count as white goods. **White goods** denote big-ticket appliances such as washers, dryers, refrigerators, etc., which all used to be white.

When stores hold after-Christmas sales, the **queues** are impossible. **Queuing** up is an art similar to standing in line (or on line, depending on where you live in the U.S.), but often there is no true line. The queue resembles a mob with each person taking his or her turn at **fronting the till** or standing in front of the cash register. A shopper needing a lay away plan will put his goods on **lay-by**. Myer, one of Australia's largest and oldest department stores, is as well known as Macy's in New York and Harrod's in London. When someone puts on airs he wears a front **as big as Myer**, meaning his actions are all a big facade!

In a department store or any other building, including a **block of units** a **flat block** or a **block of flats** (apartment house or complex), the floor above the ground floor equals the **first floor**. So if you live in the middle of a three-story house, you reside in a **first-floor flat**. Aussies never sit on a porch. They sit on **verandas**. To most Americans the veranda trims the sides of a big ranch house, and is open and airy. A porch is a porch, romantic, gracious and welcoming. But, in Australia, there is no distinction. **Veranda** even refers to petit city porches surrounded by flowers and rosebushes.

Someone may tell you they grew up on an **estate** in Oz. Don't be impressed. They mean **housing estate**, the equivalent of a housing development. While the name **terrace houses** makes these inner city dwellings sound grander than rowhouses or even brownstones, they fit the same basic concept: one- or two-story attached houses (rarely three stories in Oz). The more stylish **terraces**, built during Victoria's reign, are in demand these days, following the brownstone revival in New York and variations on the theme throughout the world. Special features in good and once-grand terrace houses are the wrought iron lacework on upper and lower balconies reminiscent of the New Orleans French Quarter and **leadlight** windows and doors. **Leadlight** replaces stained glass.

If you tell someone to wait a minute, you say "**Just a tick**," and when something will be done in a jiffy, it'll be **done in a tick!** But if you expect it a week from Friday, you can expect it **Friday week** (or **Monday week**, **Tuesday week**, etc.).

Yank Tanks

Outside the house the car plays an important role in Australian life, mainly because the country is so big and sprawling. The terms dealing with cars are very British. Aussies even drive on the left side of the road and fill their cars with **petrol**, not gasoline. The mechanic checks under the **bonnet** to make sure everything operates properly. The driver stows the spare **tyre** in the **boot** (trunk).

A **combi** is a Volkswagen bus outfitted as a combination (combi) car and camper or **campervan**. Volkswagen is commonly shortened to **vee-dub**; even "V.W." is too many syllables for the Aussies. Another recreational vehicle is a **caravan**, the kind of camper-trailer which you tow by car and then set up on site at a **caravan park**. Australians always make fun of the great big cars Americans drive, like Cadillacs and Lincolns. They call them **Yank tanks**.

The Range Rover was built as a four-wheel-drive vehicle used by the man on the land to get about. But, somewhere along the way, they became as popular as Volvo station wagons in the wealthy suburbs and took on the nickname **Toorak tractor**, after the posh Melbourne suburb.

When they talk about registration, Aussies talk about, you guessed it, the **reggo** (pronounced *rejjo*). License plates replace **reggo plates**. License is spelled *licence*, like *defence*. At this point, what else would you expect from our Aussie mates?

You don't have "fender benders" in Oz because there are no fenders per se. Instead your vehicle suffers a **prang** (an accident). The **panel beater** will put the car back in shape (as opposed to beating it more). **Panel beaters** work in the auto body shop, straightening out **mudguards** (fenders) and anything else smashed in the **prang**. Hiding in the toolbox will be a spanner. A workman reaches for a **spanner** instead of a wrench in Australia. Therefore, in colloquial speech if someone **mucks it up**, he's thrown a **spanner** in the works.

On a lighter motoring note, a family may **go for a burl** or a leisurely drive on a Sunday afternoon. They'll pack lunch and throw some soft drinks and ice in the **esky** (cooler).

Chapter 12

To Barrack or to Play

The Aussies are great outdoors people. After all, they have the kind of space few other nations can claim—only 17 million people in a country the size of the continental United States. That grants them plenty of room to spread out and have a good time. And they do! Add that space to greater leisure time. The country is based on a 37-and-a-half-hour work week, with at least six to eight paid holidays a year, plus five to six weeks paid vacation. In most cases, unused vacation time can be stored up year after year if not used. How's that? (As the Aussies tend to ask.)

Since the majority of that small population lives within an hour's drive to the ocean, all ages enjoy all sorts of water sports. As we've discovered in our travel section, yachting, swimming, diving, fishing, surfing, wind surfing (or sailboarding) and water skiing number among the most popular involvement sports.

But Aussies are also **keen** (meaning fanatical) spectators. Families watch **sport** on television, not sports. For some reason, unknown perhaps, they say **sport**, like "religion" as an all encompassing word.

Yachties

If you know anything about Australians you know

they are **mad keen yachties**, whether they actually sail or just watch. The final proof of their strength, in their eyes, was winning the America's Cup 12-metre races in Newport, Rhode Island, in 1983. And they would rather not discuss the loss on their home waters in 1987.

If yachting is your interest in Australia and you've skipped directly to this chapter hoping to be told enough about Australian-English to get you through a day on and off the waves with a crew from Down Under—sorry! You'll have to read Chapter 6 to find out what they say when they are not throwing around yachting jargon, and certainly you'll need to read Chapter 7 to find out what you'll be eating and, most of all, read Chapter 8 to learn about Aussie drinking habits so you'll know how to enjoy the victory party. Someone may offer you a **stubby** or a **pony** or invite you to **hit the turps**! Then what? You may even find yourself at a **barby** with a few **prawns** or **bangers** on the grill. Whatever the case, enjoy the merrymaking with the other **septics** and **pommies** who might have gone along too. (You'll find out what they are later.) So leave the nautical lingo to the race course (and the maritime dictionary) and concentrate on the social scene. Oh! Better check Chapter 8 to find out who **sheila** is and when to call someone a **mate**!

Surfies

As for those of you who will look beyond the yachts for a good time, you might like to be reminded of some terms that might help during your seaside stay. Miles of inviting beaches are patrolled closely by volunteer life-guards who are members of local **surf livesaving clubs** or **S.L.C.**s. The surf livesavers are the fellows and girls, men and women, who wear colored swim caps and tank tops. They are proficient not only in swimming but also in surf-skis (a cross between surfboards and kayaks with paddles) and surf lifeboats, rowed by teams through the heavy ocean waves. To prove their athletic prowess, the S.L.C. teams compete during **surf carnivals** every year, giving them a competitive reason to remain in shape. They must run, swim, row and act out saving lives for points. The surf carnival is a fun time for the town that holds it and worth being a part of, even if you're just visiting. Everyone comes out to watch.

Another entry at a carnival might be surfing competition. This water sport created another subculture in Australia and another chapter full of language. The **surfies** or **boardies** live lives reminiscent of Gidget movies and have a beach language unique to their lifestyle. Their jargon is not part of mainstream Australian-English except perhaps in beach communities. However, some words do sneak into common usage. **Boomers** are big waves anywhere. (While a **boomer** can also be a giant kangaroo.) Surfies wear **cozzies** and **board shorts** (they are long-legged surfers' swimsuits) accompanied by colorful singlets. They walk around with zinc oxide on their noses to block the sun, and thongs (rubber sandals) on their feet to protect their soles from the hot sand.

Those not game enough to take on surfing may take part in a more passive but time consuming leisure activity, sunbathing on a **lilo**. Lilo? It's a brand name for an inflatable vinyl raft. No Aussie ever talks about a raft, only a "Lie-low." Get it? They even take them camping as matresses.

On the Oval

Most Australian sports involving a ball have been handed down by the British Commonwealth, but not all of them. Cricket, of course, is English and the Aussies have adopted it as their national sport. They compete on every level from schoolboy sports to International Test Cricket, played among the Commonwealth countries. Australia's rivals include the West Indies (known as the Windies), Pakistan, India, New Zealand and

Mother England, along with African countries touched by British rule. Simply (and that's the only way I would dare to explain it), cricket is played with a bat held by a **batsman** (not a batter as in baseball). The hard ball, traditionally red in color, is pitched or **bowled** by a **bowler** (no pitcher). The **pitch** refers to the packed running surface beneath the bowler's feet. The **wicket** consists of three wooden sticks standing upright called **stumps** with two **bails** or small wooden dowels across the top. The bowler aims at the wicket and tries to knock the bails off, while the batsman tries to slap the ball away with a flat bat held low to the ground. If the bowler knocks the bails off, the batsman is out. As in baseball, the batsman can be caught out on a fly. Actually there are two batsmen on the oval (named for the shape of the field) simultaneously; but, I'll let someone else explain the nitty-gritty to you. To try to learn more without actually watching a match would be confusing.

Let me add that a **test match**, which is technically one game, continues over five days with a 40-minute lunch break and a 20-minute afternoon tea break every day. Imagine sitting from 11a.m. to 6p.m. for five consecutive days waiting for the outcome of one game! Even then it is possible to end in a draw! In these less gracious modern times, people want to see more cricket played in shorter periods of time. So, an Aussie businessman helped create **one-day cricket** played by teams dressed in colored uniforms (not the traditional sporting white). The one-day games were perfect for television but the International Test Matches will always be the most important games of the year.

The first cricket batter of the day is called the **opening batsman**. A big name batsman is as well known in Australia as Joe DiMaggio is in America. Therefore the name of a batsman gets dragged into idiomatic slang. You may hear someone at a **barby** ask, "Pass the **Colin Mc Donald**." He does not want the player handed to him, he wants a bottle opener. Colin McDonald equals opening batsman or opener! Ever heard of a **sticky wicket**? Perhaps you heard it in an old movie and wondered what on earth they were talking about and where did such a saying come from. The answer: cricket, of course! It means the ground around the wicket is wet or muddy. Now it is a euphemism for any "messy or difficult situation." A **good wicket** is just the opposite—advantageous.

In most cities you can pick the cricket oval by the initials **C.G.** They stand for **cricket ground**. Hence, they play cricket at the M.C.G. (The Melbourne Cricket Ground) or the S.C.G. (The Sydney Cricket Ground). But Brisbane will throw you. Queenslanders like being different. While they compete at a place formally named the Brisbane Cricket Ground on maps and tourist pamphlets, no one in Australia calls it that. The stadium stands in a suburb named Woolloongabba, so the cricket ground is always referred to as **The Gabba**.

Footy

Since cricket fields are rather large sporting arenas, other games and events can be played there too, including football. While Australians play rugby and soccer, there's only one game they call football, **Australian Rules football**. Colloquially, it's **Aussie rules** or just plain **footy**. Footy has been mentioned in other sections of this book because it is **dinky-di** Australian and there's no escaping it.

Because Aussie Rules bears the title "football," the Australians needed another heading for the American game. To them U.S. football with helmets and all the padded paraphenalia is **gridiron** (as in "on the gridiron"). With the exception of an egg-shaped ball and a large playing field, the two sports have very little in common. The 18 players on a footy side never stop. The game runs for 100 minutes, divided into four 25-minute quarters (which can be extended at the umpires' discretion). At the half, there is a 20-minute break. The play really never stops unless a stretcher must be brought onto the field to move an injured player. Otherwise, injuries get treated right on the field while the match continues around the man and the medic!

Footy is a winter sport, played from March through September, though to look at the uniforms you would not think so. Footy players dress like soccer and rugby players, in shorts and sleeveless jerseys, called **footy jumpers**. (Once in a while a long-sleeve rugby-style jumper will show up.) They do not wear any protective padding or headgear. That's not to say they couldn't use some protection, but it's just **not on**! Some say that would detract from the raw beauty of the play. To the untrained eye, it looks like chaos on the oval! Like American football, a team wins by scoring goals. But there are four goal posts on each end, two tall inside posts and two shorter **behind** posts. A player gets six points for a goal and one point for **behinds**. To score a goal worth six points, a player has to kick a ball clearly between the two big posts without it being touched by another player. If another player touches it or if the ball hits a post on its way through, it only scores one point.

The raucous crowds at Aussie Rules matches would not be complete without **hoons** and **larrikans** toting their share of **stubbies** and **brownies**, **tinnies**, **T.T.**'s and **tubes**. A **stubby** or a **brownie** denotes a short brown bottle. Tinnies and T.T's stem from the days when cans were made of tin, not **aluminium**. Tubes is modern slang for can. Remember you don't "root for a team" in Oz. That would make you a bit more intimate than a cheerleader. Instead, you **barrack for** a team. **Barrack** has an aboriginal history—first meaning to jeer at your enemy. Then it became synonymous with cheering for a side. In modern times, especially when it comes to

footy, you **barrack for** your favorite team and **barrack against** their opponents.

Barrackers (not rooters) don their team colors in the form of woolly hats and scarves in the winter, and other things in the summer. They end the footy season in September. Their version of the Superbowl is the **Grand Final**. The state of Victoria, home of footy, where the majority of the teams are located, goes wild! Fans suffer **Grand Final fever**!

Aussie Rules started in Victoria, where the miners in the 1850s made up a version of football, but up north the most popular winter game played on the oval remains rugby or **rugger**. But even in the rugby world confusion for the outsider exists. Two distinctly different rugby games are played: **Rugby Union** and **Rugby League**. League is the professional sport and union the school sport, closer to the British game. Just to throw another **spanner** in the works when you thought you were getting the hang of this—Queenslanders refer to rugby as **footy**.

Bowls

Careful when you talk about bowling in Australia. You may find yourself in the wrong conversation. The bowling played indoors on wooden alleys had to be renamed, just like gridiron, because of the game known as **bowls**. The American game is **ten-pin bowling**. Aussies play a version of lawn bowls imported from the British Isles. The **bowlers** (not to be confused with the cricketers and the ten-pin competitors) roll balls on grass at bowling clubs where many members are retirees or **pensioners**. This kind of bowling is similar to the Italian game of bocce, which is played only with balls, not pins or clubs. Bowlers wear sporting white from the tips of their shoes to the tops of their hats. You cannot miss them walking down the street.

Punting

While cricket fills the bill as national sport, Australia's second greatest spectator sport is horse racing. Horse racing means gambling. So really the sport is **punting**. Punters bet. Any race day is labeled a **race meeting** or a **derby** (pronounced *darby*). The race of the year is the **Melbourne Cup**. In many ways it's the equivalent of the Kentucky Derby, but unlike the Run for the Roses, Melbourne Cup Day is a state holiday. Melbourne closes down so everyone can dress up and go to Flemington Race Course. Traditionally, track members and their guests dress in their fanciest clothes and women try to outdo each other with the grandest outfits and finest hats. Every society columnist and fashion editor in the country descends on Flemington to see who is wearing what. You see, the race runs the first Tuesday in November and that may be the first glimpse of the summer fashion season.

Even if you are not a member, you can still go to Flemington and have a tailgate party in the parking lot. The folks who go do not dress in haute couture like the members; instead, they go in **fancy dress**. Fancy dress means costumes. People outdo each other with the wildest hats and headgear. Whether inside or outside the gates, the champagne flows and everyone has a wonderful time. Now, even if you are not in Melbourne for Cup Day, you can probably attend a Melbourne Cup party at a pub or racecourse which will have closed-circuit TV of the Cup races and local races as well. No one is left out.

In some places (more and more each year), casino gambling has been legalized. The favorite pastime inside the clubs can be summed up in one phrase: the **pokies.** That's the pet name for **poker machines**, better known to us as one-armed bandits or the slots.

Other Sport

Track and field events are popular, too, especially in school competitions. But, the sports category is not track and field as Americans call it. Runners compete in **athletics**.

A lefty or southpaw in Australia bears the moniker **molly-dooker**. The player, in any sport, recognized as the team's most valuable performer will be presented with the "**best and fairest**" award. It takes the place of the M.V.P.

Women play a version of basketball in Oz, called **netball**. It has seven players on each side and they pass the ball a lot like women's basketball once did. It's a popular club sport usually played on outdoor courts.

Just like American kids, Aussie boys and girls have their unofficial sports. **Billycart** racing sits atop the list like the carts do atop a hill at the starting line. **Billycarts** closely resemble homemade go-carts. Somehow **billy** edged into the seat of another word, sat down and stayed forever. After all, wouldn't it be as easy to call them just plain carts?

When not rolling along in billycarts, you will probably find kids pedaling **pushbikes**. Pushbikes do not differ from other kinds of bicycles. It's just a compound word that came from pushing pedals. So, bikes and push-bikes, carts and billycarts are two sets of twins.

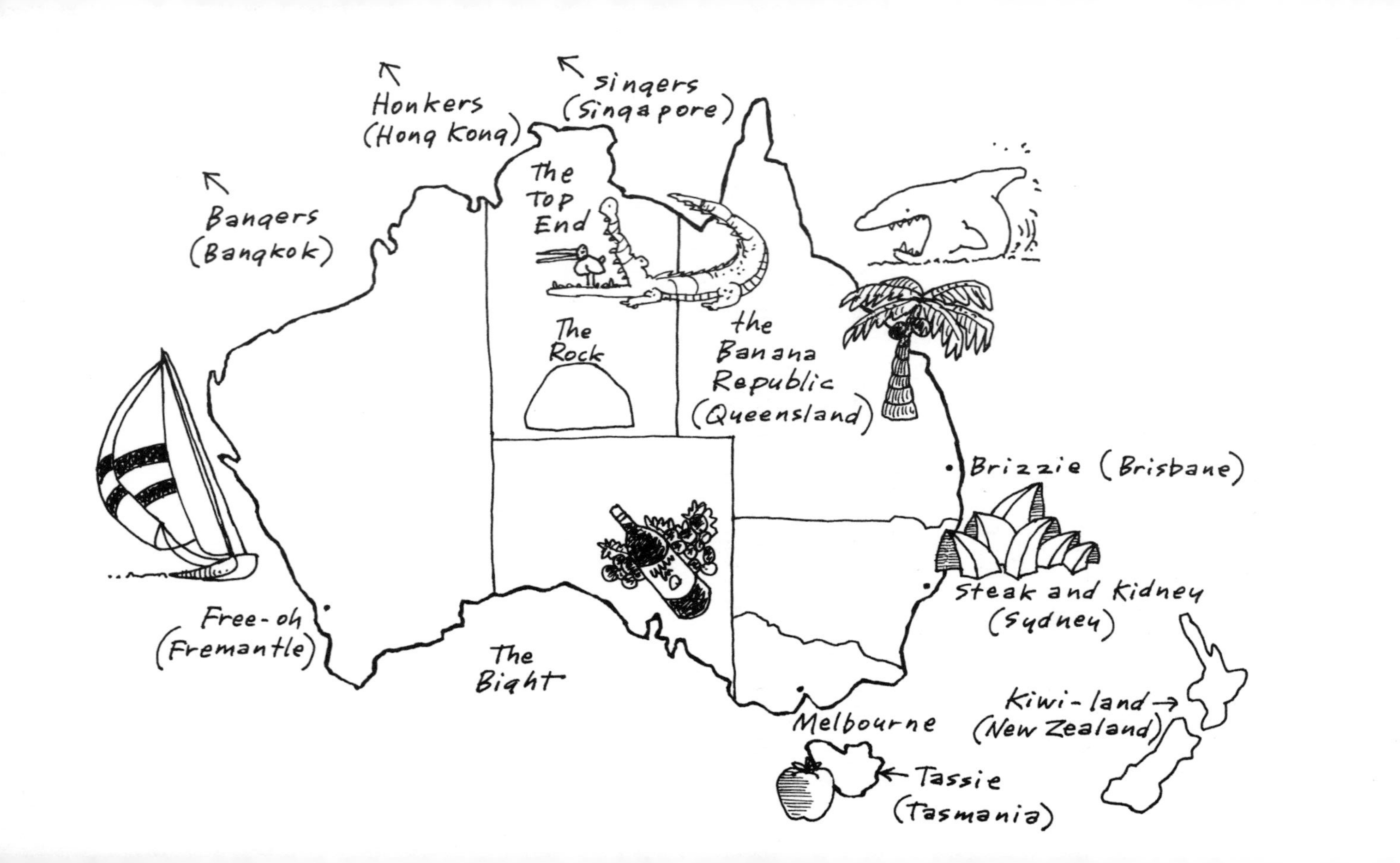
Honkers (Hong Kong)
singers (Singapore)
Bangers (Bangkok)
The Top End
The Rock
the Banana Republic (Queensland)
Brizzie (Brisbane)
Steak and Kidney (Sydney)
Free-oh (Fremantle)
The Bight
Melbourne
Kiwi-land (New Zealand)
Tassie (Tasmania)

Chapter 13

People Aussies Meet and Places Aussies Go

Aussies is the wonderful clipped version of Australians which the men and women Down Under proudly wear. It fits their style of informality. That informality carries over in their dealings with other countries and other peoples.

The general feeling that Australians "got it good" makes them a bit cocky (in the real definition of that word). Americans, for instance, have always been **Yanks**. The British called the early American colonists that and it has stuck. So the Aussies needed to create another handle for Yanks. Rhyming slang came to the rescue. Consider Americans **Septics**. What a lovely term! Have you figured it out? **Septic Tank** rhymes with **Yank**. Americans are then **Septic Tanks**, shortened to **Septics.** Perhaps at one time it was meant to be derogatory, but now it's all in fun.

Pommies are another story. All English people are called **Poms** or **Pommies** by the Aussies. The word descends from the days of convict transportation, or so legend has it. According to word-of-mouth tradition, the British subjects brought to the prison settlements of Australia were labeled "Prisoner of His Majesty" or P.O.M. But when life turned around and the Australians were guardians and rulers of their own land, they turned the ugly phrase on all other Brits still serving the crown. Now all British citizens are **Pommies**. They know it and accept it. Whether they like it is another matter. The **Macquarie Dictionary**, considered by its publishers as "an Australian achievement," and by others as the dictionary of the English language in Australia, cites the definition of **Pommy** as "an Englishman," but adds that the origin of the word remains unknown. I suppose Macquarie lexicographers don't believe the legend.

New Zealanders have been burdened with a different brand which they'll never shake either. To Australians their neighbors will always be **Kiwis**, no matter what they do. Kiwi, in any form, relates to New Zealand, just as kangaroos and koalas relate to Oz. The kiwi is a small flightless bird, native only to the islands of New Zealand, or **Kiwiland**. In modern times people might think of the kiwi fruit as the origin of the handle hung on New Zealanders; but in a sense, it's the other way around. Because kiwi is associated with New Zealand so strongly, a bright marketing manager began to push the kiwi fruit on the world market. But, there was no fruit by that name. He made it up. The kiwi fruit is the Chinese gooseberry which grows well in the New Zealand climate (and in Oz). You won't find the name kiwi fruit anywhere before the 1970s. One other phrase sometimes denotes the **Kiwi.** He might be called an **Enzed** or **Enzedder**. We are talking about New Zealanders here. *En* equals *N* and *zed* equals *Z*. Therefore, their name gets clipped to Enzed—a strange phrase. Most other slang for nationalities is degrading, usually insulting to a particular group of immigrants. Most are not much different from those thrown around the United States and therefore not worth mentioning.

A Visit to Honkers!

It may be an extension of "rock fever" that drives

Australians to travel, especially those born after World War II. It's not unusual for baby boomers to take a year or longer off from work and leave Australia by boat or plane and find what the rest of the world is doing. Because travel is a common experience, favorite locations have been given nicknames Down Under. The best ones are those close by (to them) in Southeast Asia. A trip to Singapore is a holiday in **Singers** and a visit to Bangkok, Thailand, is a visit to **Bangers**. As an example of how commonplace these terms are, an airline adopted one in its slogan for trips to Hong Kong, a favorite shopping and business destination from Australia. The ad campaign for Cathay Pacific Airline used the colloquialism this way: "You'd be bonkers not to go via **Honkers**!" Honkers replaces Hong Kong.

QANTAS

Qantas, with its kangaroo logo, is the national airline of Australia, but most foreigners do not understand the strange word Qantas. No, it is not aboriginal and they do not drop the *qu* combination in Oz. Qantas is an acronym for Queensland and Northern Territory Aerial Service. Now you know. It's a great piece of trivia with which to stump your friends.

Inside Oz

As we've said, Aussies call their own home **Oz**. Changes in the place names on maps do not stop there. Queensland, the Sunshine State, seems to bear the brunt of lots of linguistic fooling around. Queensland, being a hot state, works at a slower pace than New South Wales or Victoria, but there's plenty of work done there in the cane fields and on the pineapple and banana plantations. Because of that, Queensland stands tall as the **Banana Republic** and the people who live there must put up with the unattractive moniker **banana-**

benders. Brisbane (pronounced *Briz-bin*) is the state capital, fondly known as **Brizzie**, and Brizzie residents are aptly called **Brizzie boys** and **Brizzie girls**, usually after they've moved elsewhere.

Queensland is not alone in the nickname category. Tasmania, originally called Van Dieman's Land under colonial rule, has fallen to the rewriters of the English language too. What sounds like a diminutive for the country's smallest state is just another clipped form. Tasmania is **Tassie** (pronounced *Tazzie*), a charming island which was once a prison.

Australia's largest city is Sydney, New South Wales. That superlative does not spare it from nicknames. Sydney falls to rhyming slang, renamed **Steak and Kidney** long before anyone can remember. The residents of Sydney call themselves **Sydneysiders**. Those living within the state boundaries of New South Wales are referred to as **New South Welshmen**.

Down in Melbourne, Victoria, a town that has never been given a nickname, people call themselves **Melburnians** and they pride themselves on their individual lifestyle distinct from that of Sydneysiders. Anyone living in that state takes on the name **Victorian**, though there may be nothing prim or prudish about him.

Any large city retains the old-fashioned title **the big smoke**. That goes back to the early years of horsemen. While still a great distance away they could spot a city on the horizon by the smoke rising above it.

Australia's west and east coasts are divided by three thousand miles of desert known as the known as the Nullarbor Plain (meaning "null arbor" or without trees). There on the other side of the continent, other destinations refuse to be left without an odd bit of local trivia. Along the coast of Western Australia, you may hear people talk about **the Doctor**. He arrives promptly every afternoon and stirs the place up. The so-called **Doctor** is neither man nor beast. The Doctor refers to the wind that blows in from the Indian Ocean everyday at lunchtime. The wind was dubbed the Doctor because of its cooling, healing effect against the strong West Australian sun. But, while the Doctor does calm the temperature, he also blows the sand around, making the beautiful endless stretches of beaches unpleasant at times. The Doctor is notorious among sailors because the strong onshore wind makes for heavy conditions and some of the world's most exciting yacht racing.

As you have learned in the section on Perth's beaches and other material written about Perth in recent years, yachting history was made in West Australia in 1987 when a tiny port town, the stepchild of Perth, became the site of the first non-American America's Cup race. The place is **Free-oh**! That is the loving pseudonym for the town of Fremantle. The clipped sobriquet was in place long before competing sailors from around the world arrived to turn the sleepy little port into an international tourist haven. Funny, though, how **Free-oh** seems to fit the spirit of the place in modern times!

In the travel section, we explained **the Outback**. Australia's heartland is a dry red center, desert and scrub. But in recent years, the Outback has come to refer to Australia's wilderness which is not all sand and heat. Now adventurers divide the Outback into two sections: **The Red** and **The Green**. Red connotes the desert region and Green befits the tropical outback, home of the rain forests, crocodiles and other beasts.

The venomous beasts of Oz are simply known as **nasties** (*nah-stees*). They can be **stingers**, the lethal box jellyfish or sea wasps, or the poisonous sea snake which roams the Great Barrier Reef.

Endnotes

While traveling in Australia it helps to be familiar with colloquialisms so you are not left in the linguistic cold during a conversation, watching a news bulletin or television sit com.

Now that you have read about the places to go, the things to see, people to meet and expressions to use, do not worry about memorizing the Aussie words. Australians will not expect a visiting Yank to turn a dinky-di Aussie phrase. Remember they understand you probably better than you understand them.

If by the end of your stay Down Under, Aussie phrases begin to roll off your tongue comfortably, use them. Just do not abuse them by forcing an accent or too many expressions. It will sound fake and Aussies will cut you to the quick for putting on a front. If someone does take the mickey out of you, laugh along and the whole moment will pass with "no worries, mate."

Bibliography

The research for any book includes a mix of sources: some spoken, some current as in periodicials and pamphlets, some historic and out-of-print. So rather than including a textbook bibliography, this abbreviated listing offers titles for further reading on Australian language and Australia in general. Most of them contributed to the research of this book, some more than others. Some may be harder to find than others, but generally they remain available in America. Minor Australian titles have been left out for the most part. The Library of the Australian Consulate in New York and the Australian Embassy in Washington may be able to help those readers doing further research.

Baker, Sidney. *The Australian Language*, Second Edition. Sydney: Currawong Publishing Company, 1966.

____. *Australia Speaks*. Sydney: Shakespeare Head Press, 1953.

____. *A Dictionary of Australian Slang*, 1982 Edition. South Yarra, Victoria: O'Neil Publishers.

Hughes, Robert. *The Fatal Shore*. New York: Alfred A. Knopf, 1987.

Jonsen, Helen. *Kangaroo's Comments & Wallaby's*

Words: The Aussie Word Book. New York: Hippocrene Books, Inc., 1988.

Macquarie University. *The Macquarie Dictionary of Australian Colloquial Language.* (1988).

____. *The Macquarie Dictionary.* (1981) Macquarie University, New South Wales: The Macquarie Library Pty. Ltd.

Newman, Graeme and Tamsin. *Hippocrene Companion Guide to Australia.* New York: Hippocrene Books, Inc., 1992.

Partridge, Eric. *A Dictionary of Slang.*

____. *A Dictionary of Slang and Unconventional English.* Hammondsworth, England: Penguin Books Ltd., 1977.

Wilkes, G.A. *A Dictionary of Australian Colloquialisms.* Australia: Fontana/Collins, 1985.

Index

The states and territories of Australia are abbreviated next to listings of cities and towns. They are as follows:

Australian Capital Territory (ACT)
New South Wales (NSW)
Northern Territory (NT)
Queensland (Qld)
South Australia (SA)
Tasmania (Tas)
Victoria (Vic)
Western Australia (WA)

In addition, rhyming slang words and phrases carry the added note (RS) next to them for easy recognition.

Hippocrene Insider's Guide to Java and Bali

by Jerry LeBlanc

The pristine beauty of Java and Bali, two of the most elegant and popular islands of Indonesia, has been compared to that of Hawaii fifty years ago. Smoking volcanoes, wild game preserves, storybook temples, palaces and markets speak of the persistence of age-old traditions even as modern skyscrapers of teeming cities rise out of tropical rainforests.

With photographs, maps, and sample itineraries, this book is a wealth of information at your fingertips. The author knows the region well—major cities, villages, natural splendor, and developed resort areas, as well as neighboring islands, are detailed. Local customs, festivals, and exquisite arts and crafts are highlighted to illustrate the colorful diversity of the jewels of Indonesia.

222 pages • $14.95 • ISBN 0-7818-0037-4
maps, photos, outlines of other Indonesian Islands

Namibia: The Independent Traveler's Guide

Scott and Lucinda Bradshaw

This in-depth, up-to-date travel guide is the only exclusive guide to be published since the changes brought about by Namibia's independence. Namibia is an exciting new destination in southwest Africa; since its independence in 1990, it is now much easier to see wildlife and unspoiled wilderness.

As Namibia is twice the size of California, this travel guide will be a necessity to make one's way around the country's vast expanses. Geared for travelers of any means, it covers eating, lodging and camping as well as sights, both on and off the beaten track. A brief listing of native languages is added. All four geographic sections are well-covered: the Namib Desert, the Great Escarpment (a semi-arid, grassy, mountainous plateau), the lower north- and southeastern lands, and the northern plains. As exotic as it is contemporary, Namibia is a colorful country with plenty of experiences waiting.

278 pages • $16.95 • ISBN 0-7818-0254-7 • maps, drawings, photos